Through Red, Gold & Green

THROUGH RED, GOLD & GREEN SPECTACLES

Articles, Essays & a Short Story

by
BARBARA MAKEDA BLAKE-HANNAH

© Barbara Makeda Blake Hannah

PUBLISHED October 1, 2023
37 Waterworks Circuit,
Kingston 8, Jamaica
jamediapro@hotmail.com

ISBN: 9798859029686

ABOUT THE AUTHOR

Barbara Makeda Blake-Hannah is a Jamaican author, journalist, film-maker and cultural consultant. She trained as a journalist in Jamaica, then emigrated to London and worked as a free lance journalist, and as PR executive for the Jamaica Tourist Board and Government. She became the first Black TV journalist in the UK in 1968 on the THAMES TV program "TODAY with Eamonn Andrews" (London) and ATV Today (Birmingham) and as a producer on BBC-TV's 'Man Alive".

In 1972, Barbara Blake-Hannah returned to Jamaica and continued writing articles and books, becoming a Rastafari and articulate campaigner for the religion, for slavery reparations and becoming known as a pioneer advocate for home-schooling. Her books include "Rastafari – the New Creation", the first book on the religion written by a Rastafari. In 1984 she was appointed an Independent Opposition Senator, becoming the first Rastafari to sit in the Jamaican Parliament.

In 2001 Mrs. Blake-Hannah served as a member of the Jamaican delegation to the UN World Conference Against Racism & Xenophobia held in Durban, South Africa, where she was a member of the special plenary on Reparations. Returning to Jamaica, she established the Jamaica Reparations movement that led to the establishment of the Government's National Council on Reparations in 2008.

Mrs. Blake Hannah has served the Rastafari Nation as a writer, film maker and spokesperson for more than 50 years. She worked as Cultural Liaison when the Jamaican Ministry of Culture, Gender, Entertainment & Sport was assigned in 2017 to administer reparations to Rastafari for the Coral Gardens Incident. Other projects in that job have included co-ordinating the Official Visit to Jamaica of Emperor Haile Selassie's grandson, H.I.H. Prince Ermias Sahle-Selassie for the National Heroes Week celebrations of Jamaica's 60th Anniversary

In 2020 the British Press Gazette established an Award named after her for Black and Ethnic Minority journalists. In 2022 Penguin Books UK published her biography "GROWING OUT- Black Hair & Black Pride in the Swinging Sixties", an account of her years in Britain and the racism that ended her career and encouraged her return to Jamaica. In 2018 she was awarded the Jamaican Order of Distinction, and in 2023 the Ethiopian Crown Council appointed her an Officer of the Order of the Star of Ethiopia.

Mrs. Blake-Hannah lives in Jamaica with her son Makonnen, who made world history when he was appointed Youth Technology Consultant to the Jamaican Government at the age of 13 years. She declares him as her greatest Blessing.

Through Red, Gold & Green Spectacles 5

CHAPTERS

MARCUS GARVEY DAY	6
RASTAFARI – THE NEW CREATION	8
BOB MARLEY – JUST A FRIEND I USED TO KNOW	12
I NEVER SWAM AT BOB MARLEY BEACH	21
TRIBUTE TO DOUGIE MACK	28
RASTAFARI ROOTZFEST	33
REPORT ON THE MISSION TO AFRICA	39
THE EMANCIPATION PARK STATUE	54
THE ISLANDER – MY LIFE IN MUSIC	67
NO MORE RASTAS	74
JAMAICA'S REGGAE FILMS	81
TELL ME SOMETHING GOOD	89
RASTAFARI – JAMAICA'S NEXT NATIONAL HERO	95
WHAT DOES AFRICA MEAN TO RASTAFARI	103
THE CORAL GARDENS INCIDENT	109
REPARATIONS – DURBAN WCAR	138
REPARATIONS – J.A.R.M.	145
TO DAMN WITH FAINT PRAISE	153
THE STORY OF MR. JONES	160
H.I.M. EMPEROR HAILE SELASSIE I	210

MARCUS GARVEY DAY - AUGUST 17, 2023

    The choice of Marcus Mosiah Garvey as Jamaica's first National Hero has never been the subject of controversy. The work and words of the man who created the Universal Negro Improvement Association as the first international organization of descendants of African slaves in North America and the Caribbean, were ample proof of Garvey's right to receive that special honor. Garvey's right to declare himself Provisional President of Africa was also not questioned by those who looked forward to him ultimately achieving that ambition to lead all of Africa's children.

    Marcus Garvey's Philosophy & Opinions collected and published by his wife Amy Jacques, have provided a treasure trove of advice, opinion and history for the Black people of the Americas and inspired us to excel in making a better life for ourselves and our race, wherever in the world we live. Garvey's words and achievements show why he has been hailed continually as one of the most important Black men to have ever lived.

    The fact that all this honor and tribute is given to a man born in humble circumstances in St. Ann, Jamaica, has elevated Garvey still further as an example for citizens of his home country. Jamaicans are forever proud of the fact that their countryman rose to inspire millions while he lived, and even more millions today when he is only with us in words and spirit.

    Garvey's Back-to-Africa movement inspired a desire for Africans to forge a link between the Caribbean and the Americas to Africa, and while his dream of repatriation to Liberia did not materialize, the call for retribution for the crime against humanity that took us from our African homeland continues to be made for Reparations to be paid by former enslavers to descendants of the enslaved.

Garvey used the trumped-up charges that were used to discredit and deport him from the United States, to fuel his effort to participate in Jamaican municipal and national politics. He expanded his activities to the creative arts, and influenced many with his fiery rhetoric. But the racial prejudices of post-colonial Jamaica conspired against Garvey and he turned his back on Jamaica, moving to England where he breathed his last breath.

Garvey's death did not end Garvey's influence. His life and work continue to encourage a sense of self-pride and worth among Africans wherever we live in the African Diaspora, inspiring the Black Power Movement and Nation of Islam in the United States, and — most fundamentally of all — the birth and growth of the RasTafari movement of Jamaica that is now a global cultural movement for people of all races.

As Garvey's birthday is celebrated in an annual national Holiday on August 17th, Jamaicans offer tributes that shine his celestial star even higher as we repeat his words of inspiration that defy racism and demand a world of equality and ONE LOVE.

> *"Men and women of Liberty Hall, men and women of my race, do you know that the God we love, the God we adore, the God who sent His Son to this world nearly two thousand years ago never created an inferior man? That God we love, that God we worship and adore has created man in His own image, equal in every respect, wheresoever he may be; let him be white; let him be yellow; let him be red; let him be black; God has created him the equal of his brother.*
>
> *He is such a loving God. He is such a merciful God. He is such a God that He is no respecter of persons, that He would not in His great love create a superior race and an inferior one. The God that you worship is a God that expects you to be the equal of other men. The God that I adore is such a God and He could be no other."* -
>
> **Hon. Marcus Mosiah Garvey, National Hero**

RASTAFARI - THE NEW CREATION

(My first book - Excerpt from Chapter One)

The RastafarI movement grew out of the darkest depression that the descendants of African slaves in Jamaica have ever lived in -- the stink and crumbling shacks of zinc and cardboard that the tattered remnants of humanity built on the rotting garbage of the dreadful Dungle on Kingston's waterfront. Out of this filth and slime arose a sentiment so pure, so without anger, so full of love, the Philosophy of the RastafarI faith.

It was a flower in a pigsty, watered by the nourishment of the Prophet Marcus Garvey, swayed by the wind of local political change, and cherished by the Black man's long-withheld desire to hold his head upright.

Freedom of Spirit, Freedom from Slavery and Freedom of Africa, was its cry.

HAIL! JAH RASTAFARI!

Leonard Barrett, a student at the University of Puerto Rico in 1968 published what was to become the first study of Rastafari. From him can be obtained an account of early I-story:

"The decade beginning 1930 and ending in 1939 may well be called the decade of despair for the average Jamaican. The political situation was stagnant. The country was still in the

hands of men who had little or no feeling for the hungry masses. The average wage for a full day of unskilled labour was twenty-five cents for men and fourteen cents for women. The island was the reserve of a few Englishmen who had the final word in all political and economic affairs. The men who invested in Jamaica did so only for monetary gains, unconcerned with human or cultural matters.

"None of the economic institutions were organized democratically. The typical institutional pattern was hierarchical, decision and direction at the apex, submission and obedience at the bottom, without the machinery whereby the masses could exert influence upon, much less control, leadership. These were the years of the Great Depression, which saw lines of hungry people. These were also the years of violent hurricanes which had left Jamaica and other West Indian islands devastated.

"These and other conditions brought only gloom and hopeless despair to thousands of Jamaicans who saw no hope of relief from their condition."

This is how RastafarI was born.

Every man looks for God in his life. Some look through various religious philosophies and never find one that answers his questions. Some civilizations have worshiped God in one of His many physical manifestations -- the Sun, the Wind, the Moon.

"The coronation of this African King (Selassie) caused some men of African descent both in Jamaica and New York to study their Bibles and the teachings of Garvey more closely. Prominent among the Jamaicans were Leonard Howell, Joseph Hibbert, Archibald Dunkley, Paul Earlington, Vernal Davis, and Ferdinand Ricketts. These Jamaicans became the pillars of the RastafarI movement, while their counterparts in New York City became the founders of the Ethiopian World Federation.

The belief of Haile Selassie as divine is believed to have been first introduced into Jamaica by Mr. Leonard Howell. Born in Jamaica, Mr. Howell had traveled widely. He had been a soldier in the Ashanti War of 1896 and is said to have spoken several African languages. He had also traveled in the United States and while there had come into contact with racism between Blacks and Whites.

"Archibald Dunkley who also claimed to have brought the doctrine to Jamaica, devoted two and a half years to the study of the Bible trying to determine whether or not Haile Selassie I was the Messiah of whom Marcus Garvey spoke. Dunkley opened a mission in Kingston in 1933 and began to preach Ras Tafari as God, the King of Kings and Root of David."

To them, the most powerful Biblical proof of their teachings was Revelation 5, Verses 1-5:

"And I saw a strong angel proclaiming with a great voice:
Who is worthy to open the book and to lose the seals thereof? And one of the elders saith unto me, Weep not; Behold the Lion of the tribe of Judah, the Root of David, hath prevailed to open the book and to lose the seven seals thereof."

These men declared as their Creed: ***Let the hungry be fed, the naked clothed, the sick nourished; the aged protected, and the infants cared for.***
Their Motto:
ONE LOVE, ONE HEART, ONE AIM, ONE DESTINY

BOB MARLEY - JUST A FRIEND I USED TO KNOW

Jamaica GLEANER - - June 1981

Bob Marley was a remarkable Black man, the kind that occurs unfortunately too infrequently in the history of the African Diaspora. Speaking as a Black Woman, there are so few who represent the free Black man -- not slave -- that when we meet one we must pause to reflect on just how truly great a Black man can be.

I made my first visit to 56 Hope Road in 1972 just after returning from living in England, where my last job was doing the PR for the international launch of Chris Blackwell and Perry Henzell's film *"The Harder They Come"*. Bob had just been signed to Island Rcords to produce the first, sensational album 'Catch A Fire' and Blackwell asked me to show some American journalists around Kingston and to meet the new artists he had just signed. That was Bob Marley and from that day's introduction I became a friend.

He and the Wailers were sitting like wet chickens on the steps leading to ther apartment upstairs the garage of 56 Hope Road, which was then their headquarters for many months before they moved into the big house in front. Though they seemed out of place and ill at ease in their surroundings, the fire of their spirit and their rebellious anger smouldered behind their quiet faces. Bob was an unforgettable personality. I did my job showing the journalists around Kingston, then continued on my urgent, personal quest to discover and become Rastafari, as I watched Bob evolve from those early days.

In 1974 I met the Wailers again while I was organizing the first Jamaica Film Festival and on the recommendation of my advisors, tried to hire the Wailers to perform at our Awards ceremony. Though our budget did not allow us to hire them eventually, my friendship continued with Bob and his brethren. I argued in print the Wailers right to their first big fee, the Jackson Five Show, when a late start caused the Jacksons to perform first and Bob and the Wailers then entertained a packed Stadium crowd till four in the morning.

And like many others, I hung around 56 Hope Road whenever I could, just to be among the peaceful, beautiful vibrations of Rastafari that encircled everyone radiating from Bob's center. When I worked at the Office of the Prime Minister that was just within walking distance, I would stop there on my way home and soak up the Rasta energy that filled the space. Bob's brethren milled around the yard, visitors came and went, music was always playing. It was a constant spectacle full of LOVEing vibrations.

Bob came to consider me a good friend and I was close enough to have been in the studio one day when he was recording *"I'm A Black Survivor"* with his wife Rita. At one point Bob took a break, sat down on the floor beside a stool I was sitting on and fell asleep. I was surprised, but felt very honoured that he was comfortable enough with me to do that. Someone woke him up after a short nap and when he jumped up, I felt like a little lion had leapt out of my lap. Bob's spirit? Who knows.

I was never a girlfriend, and as I knew that Bob had many affairs, I avoided that kind of friendship. One Saturday afternoon he and his best friend Allan 'Skill' Cole stopped by my flat and did their best to persuade me and a girlfriend to accompany them to Cane River Falls, where they would go regularly to wash their locks and enjoy some time in the wild river valley. But I was aware of the intimacy that I knew would follow if I accompanied them, I turned down the offer and continued being just a friend.

As I was now growing as a Rasta, I and friends like myself enjoyed being around Bob and the new musical experience that was happening with him as its chief guru. It was very good for my education as a Rasta to be among all the irie friends who hung around the old Hope Road mansion in the early years. Those were good times when Bob would relax by strumming his guitar under the ackee tree in the backyard.

I remember one evening when Bob and his bredrin were reasoning with some fragrant cool herbs and enjoying life. Bob just picked up his guitar and said to Dermot Hussey, who hosted a popular radio program: "Hear some new songs I'm working on..." and just started to play, song after song, music after music, some complete, some just snatches, music flowing out of Bob like pure water flowing from a river.

When we all just listened and marveled in quiet admiration, but Bob just smiled and shrugged off the praise that followed, saying: *"Not I, but the Most High in I"*.

It's a phrase I've never forgotten and used often since then, because it says exactly where anything worth praising comes from. I don't know which songs they were, or if any of them ever became songs we know. But it was just a very special moment as the dusk shadows dropped on a beautiful Rasta evening.

Sometimes Bob would kick some ball on the front lawn that was now a dusty yard because of all the ball Bob kicked there. There would be maybe five or six other friends playing, usually with Skill Cole among them, but Bob was a one-man team, everybody else was the other team and his team mus' win. Bob played hard and it was fun to watch him playing. Everyone would be laughing, watching him play.

It was like being in the presence of a Holy Man, yet Bob had no airs and never changed from being just a down-to-earth, feet-in-the-dust man -- Christ-like, is the analogy that comes to mind.

It wasn't always easy for me to keep visiting, as the business grew and became formalized and managers became over-protective, but I continued to stop by whenever I could. Moreover, as woman, Rasta-woman, African-woman -- a friends-only relationship is a finely-balanced and delicate entity, preserved only by discretion and respect.

As he became more famous and, especially after the attempted murder before the '*Smile Jamaica*' concert when the dangers of his existence became obvious, the casual moments around Bob became fewer, but Bob was always glad to see me.

There was the afternoon when I came to tell him that my proposal the he be given the Keys to the City had been turned down by the then-City Fathers. Bob just shrugged and said "Never mind. I only said Yes because it was you who asked me, Barbara. Babylon mus' burn!"

For Bob was accustomed to rejection from an administration whose highest house of culture -- the Institute of Jamaica -- had never seen fit to award him an honour, not even when they gave out 500 Centenary Medals. Bob - a prophet without honour in his own country until he lay on his deathbed.

It was the last time I saw Bob. He had some visitors, a famous Black American musician who was in awe of meeting Bob,

(I forget his name). Then he played some football, Bob as usual against the rest of the men on the field, and Bob as usual the BEST player on the field. Then he sat down to rest and read from the autobiography of Emperor Haile Selassie.

"You read this yet, Barbara?" he asked. I had not. "What?" he was astonished, but smiling. "You fi read it, Sis. Knowledge and wisdom in dis book!" When I eventually said I had to leave, he called someone and told him to drive me home. "Carry her whichever part she wan' go!" were his instructions to the man, and the last words I ever heard from Bob.

Bob attracted by being a warrior for the cause of Justice and the rights of the still-poor children of slaves. This gave him an aura more powerful than that which is based on popular fame or sensuality, for it created Perfect Love between Bob and the millions in tune with his Divine Vibrations.

These vibrations emanated from his songs which touched chords in the hearts, memories and wombs of us Black women, lyrics which we could only feel but not express as we -- from a distance, from a memory stretching back through our mother's mother -- remembered the pain we had suffered when our fathers, daughters, sons and lovers were taken from us, as we worked endlessly for No Pay, Low Pay, Lie Down Pay, Suck Salt Pay. As we took on the beauty standards of another race's women in an attempt to win the favour of our masters, and those of our men who loved our master's women.

Like Garvey before him, Bob helped us free ourselves from those pains and replace them with the joys of being a part of a New Creation of Black Madonnas, of a new African-ness, cleansed with a new vision, a wider breadth and a richer strength. That vision encompassed a view of a Black warrior, bearing not a spear or a gun, but the peaceful music of Love -- Love of Black Man, Love of Black Woman, Love of Black People and Love of All People. The Prince of Peace, the total Rastaman.

Who could help loving him, who heard his Psalms of Love, Righteousness and the inevitability of Black Redemption. Only the wicked hated him, for his words made them uneasy and they feared the sight of his locks, the mark of warrior which he wore like the Mau Mau of Kenya before him.

And like them, he too was a guerilla warrior, but his weapons were the words of his songs -- hatred of downpression, anger at poverty, the injustice of slavery, the need for Repatriation (whether actual or simply cultural and spiritual), the love of GodJAH and the recognition of one's Divine Spirit.

In his last year, Bob's spiritual emphasis broadened to include Garvey and Christ, even being baptized in the Ethiopian Orthodox Church in the name of Christ. "Africa in ten years time? Africa will be dreadlocks -- Christ's Government will rule," he said in an interview broadcast on the day of his death.

Yes, JAH would never give the power to a baldhead, and the message had come instead in the sweetest, Blackest and most divine form -- words of song from a man who had experienced the Christ example through a Black King on an African throne. And though we may crucify the dread, time alone will tell that it was not wrong to see the Conquering Lion of the Tribe of Judah as the Christ reborn for the Black Man and Woman today. For in seeing H.I.M., a lot of people tried to live Life right, in a Christly way, in the name of JAH RASTAFARI.

Bob was human also, flesh with weaknesses like David, who he was in another incarnation. But whatever his fleshy weaknesses, they are in the dust, while Bob's message is everliving, continuing for years and years and years.

And the message Bob lived, sang and died to show us was the truths of Marcus Garvey, Haile Selassie and Iyesos Christ in an African way, for all the peaceful Black warriors of today, and for all Mankind. For Ethiopia shall truly stretch forth her hands unto God, and we are the Ethiopians.

Peace & Love, Bob. You have earned your place in Zion.

I NEVER SWAM AT BOB MARLEY BEACH

Facebook — April 2023

    I never swam at Bob Marley beach. In the past, what is today known as Bob Marley Beach was just the sea and sand beside the road to a Rasta community at Nine Miles. There the sea began with a sharp and immediate drop from where the sand ended, deep enough that the fishermen could step straight from the sand into their boats and start rowing right away, not have to push out a long way first. In fact, it was a little dangerous to swim there because of that.

    It was just a fisherman's beach, nothing more. Just the seaside beside the dirt track from the main road, where everything came to a stop under Macca trees at the simple Rasta dwellings that were all that was there. It wasn't a big community — just a few tents, a dwelling or two of sheets of zinc, weather-beaten plywood, some canvas, some blue plastic, some bamboo, some thatch. Underneath those shelters lived a few of the original real Rasta people, surviving in the typical Rasta fashion of bygone days 50 years ago.

    I was then a very early student of Rasta history and lifestyle. I had just returned from 8 years in England, determined to live my life as close to Rastafari as I could. I had a one-bedroom flat in a larger house at Bay View, a hillside of middle-class houses overlooking the road between Seven and Nine Miles on the road to St. Thomas.

50 years ago, when I wanted a sea bath, I would go to Cable Hut or Brooks Pen at Nine Miles, where I would find beaches with a gentle sloping sea floor and quiet waves, where I had a place to sit under shelter, with rooms to change clothes and a shower to wash off the salt water and the sand… those were the beaches on the coast at Nine Miles. I would buy a bun-and-cheese and soft drink, swim and laze in the sun.

But whenever I wanted to buy some ganja and smoke it undisturbed by Police and people, I would buy some extra groceries, let the bus carry me one stop further than usual, and disembark at the stop near the start of the track to the Binghi. There I would buy a piece of ice at the bar to add to my bag of groceries, then start walking down the road past the seaside.

There were only bushes and Macca trees giving shelter on the hill side of the stony track, but the sea would provide a lovely view on the other side, so I could avert my eyes as I passed Bunny Wailer's house if his wife happened to be sitting on her verandah. She had mental health problems and was sometimes "off", so I wouldn't want to disturb her with a look or even a word as I passed by. I never saw Bob visiting. Also living in that community was 'Ital' Stewart, the footballer. He and Allan 'Skill" Cole were two very famous Jamaicans. Footballers were more famous than reggae artists in those days, and Bob and the Wailers were not yet famous.

Soon I would be at Iyah Fuzzy's one-room dwelling, unpacking my little bag of vegetables, some rice, some red peas, some limes and especially the piece of Ice for him to make ice cold lemonade. He loved ice cold lemonade. Inside the little room was a bed, a small table with a Bible on it, and I could see a chimmy under the bed. I would avert my eyes and look instead at the uniform hanging on the wall with a militant decoration on the chest. I was too early a beginner in the study of Rastafari history to know that this man was a senior warrior in the epic battle against Babylon, and that he had worn that uniform on many occasions, especially the one in which he unfurled the flag of Ethiopia in the House of Parliament.

He told me about it. "Astonishment took hold of them," Fuzzy laughs. "Policeman frighten, and grab me." Madame Rose Leon, a prominent politician of the time, came with two lawyers to pay his fine. She thought he had done nothing wrong.

Why did he do it? "Does not the House represent us? So, what is the flag that represents us? (At that time the red, white and blue Union Jack of Britain represented Jamaica). "You cannot have Black people not represented by a Black flag." That was Fuzzy's simple logic.

When he came before the judge, the judge said wearily: " I don't know what to do with these people, for they are going to mash up this Government. I am only sorry that I don't have the money to charter a ship, and it is too far for them to swim it across." Fuzzy roars with laughter to tell the story. "You can go," said the judge, "but don't go back there again." His eyes twinkle like a little boy's.

The uniform served to remind him of the history he had made and he was glad to have me as an audience, as not many people remembered Iya Fuzzy or his story. To him I was just an uptown girl abandoning her middle-class upbringing to transform herself into a Rasta woman. There were only a few of us in those days.

I got to know some of the residents of the Rasta community. There was Norma Hamilton, another middle-class girl like me who I had known while growing up. She had worked as a journalist, but now she had become Farika Birhan, her Rasta name to which was later added the title 'Nana" or Queen Mother. Sister Farika had one son growing with her there, who is now a university professor of maths and technology. She later moved to live in America, where she did great Rasta work with the African Union and was recently awarded a US Presidential Medal for her service to the Afro-American community. She had two sons 20 years later who became friends with my own young son when she sent them to stay with us at our house in Portland.

Another friend on the beach was Bongo Shephan. There is a well-known photo of him earnestly kneeling to speak with Emperor Haile Selassie who was presenting him with a Gold Medal during his 1966 visit to Jamaica. Years later Bongo Shephan helped organize the Smithsonian Museum Exhibition of Rastafari culture and led the delegation of 23 brethren and sisters who traveled to the USA in 2009 to present it, with workshops and speeches about the movement in Washington, DC and several other cities. Bongo Shephan did many other great works for Rastafari from his base at that Nine Miles community, traveling to the Caribbean and the wider world spreading the philosophy and earning the title of 'Rastafari Ambassador' for his work.

My best friend was Sister Bubbles, an elder Rasta woman who would always come over to sit and talk to me. She was the only roots Rasta woman I had ever met, and she would tell me how to be a Rasta woman in dress, behavior and attitude. She explained to me why the women of the community wore slips or below-the-knees dresses when they wanted to splash in the sea, saying that modesty was imperative for women around Rasta men who were not their partners. "The women don't want to raise up the sap in strange men', she said, 'by exposing their bodies in public'. She showed me passages in the Bible about womanhood, and especially Proverbs 31: "Who can find a virtuous woman?"

When I told her that I had got a job at Michael Manley's Office of the Prime Minister, she was very happy. "Now you can grow your dreadlocks, Sister Makeda," was her immediate cry. I smiled. But I was not yet brave enough to add dreadlocks to the sandals, skirt and head-covering wrap that made me stand out while I ignored the frowning looks from some of the OPM staff and officials.

Sister Bubbles had the most beautiful singing voice I had ever heard, crystal clear with an ability to harmonize that was unique. It was always a special joy to hear her sing out above the Nyahbinghi drumming and chanting that usually began as night was falling and it was time for me to find my way home. I am so glad that her vocal addition to the chants has been captured for eternity on the album *"Churchical Chants of the Nyahbinghi"* that I can play whenever I want to nourish my spiritual vibes. Sister Bubbles is gone in flesh now, but she lives forever on a YouTube link to the album. Bongo Sheffan is gone now too, he did his work and left his mark.

I haven't been down that dirt track for more than 20 years. The last time was when a great Nyahinghi was held there that was historic, because for the first time the Boboshanti from the EABIC camp up the hill on the other side of the main road were allowed to come down and join the Binghi without having to remove their turbans. It had never happened before, and it made a wonderful unity of two Rastafari mansions on a beautiful full moon night.

I remember Elder Empress Ma Shanti telling me that night in whispered tones that her doctor had told her that the best way to cure her terrible neck pain was to remove some of her lengthy and heavy dreadlocks, and asking what I thought of her doing that. I told her that hair was only dead cells, like fingernails, and she should do as the doctor advised. Years later she met me at another Binghi with shorter dreadlocks and a smile of thanks.

As I read this week's news about 'Bob Marley Beach' that used to be the fisherman's rest I used to walk past, I smile at the thought of how Bongo Sheffan would have shouted at the girls in string bikinis sunning near-naked bodies on the black sand. "Fiya Bun Babylon!" he would have shouted at what Rastas of his time considered an immodest display. Not so today. When I questioned the bare-headed, pants-wearing attire of a young woman described as 'Rasta', whose angry run-in with Police resulted in her arrest and subsequent loss of dreadlocks, I was told by one of today's outspoken Rastas "This is modern times. Women can wear what they want - Rasta is not the Taliban!"

I never swam in the sea beside the road to the Rasta's camp at what is now called 'Bob Marley Beach' but I will do that one day soon. Children and grandchildren of the people I knew 50 years ago have grown up now under the Macca trees and I am sure the spirits of Bongo Sheffan, Nana Farika and Sister Bubbles are surely still there. I hope they, and their contribution to Rastafari history, will forever be remembered and glorified.

-

TRIBUTE TO DOUGIE MACK

(*Delivered at: Memorial to Bro. Douglas Mack, Institute of Jamaica, May 21, 2023*)

I came home to Jamaica in 1972 interested in the political potential of Rastafari's Afrocentric philosophy as a way to build a new Jamaica. But there was little instruction among the uptown people whom I was supposed to mix with, who were all espousing the philosophy of Democratic Socialism. I searched among them in vain to try to get to know more about Rastafari.

So I struck out into the unknown. I said to a Rasta man I met on the fringe of one of the political meetings: "I want to become a Rasta."

He looked at me to see if I was serious, then said: "I will take you to the teachers."

He drove me down to East Kingston, to Slip Dock Road off Windward Road where he picked up a man with a saxophone who he introduced as Tommy McCook. Then he drove further East up to Wareika Hill, to the Glasspole Avenue home of Brother Dougie Mack, my first Rasta teacher, who was to become the foundation of my knowledge of the history and livity of Rastafari.

This was the place I came to call "HEAVEN", where some of my good friends used to live. It was not a place many people could visit – the people who lived in HEAVEN were very choosy about who they allowed to come there.

HEAVEN was a colony of dwellings on the hillside of Wareika, the
notorious haven of the poor and criminals, where Rastafari bloomed after its escape from the razing of the West Kingston "Dungle", or dung hill, where they had made their humble homes.

HEAVEN was the place where Count Ossie first started beating his Rasta drums to create the Mystic Revelation of Rastafari.

HEAVEN was the place the police continually busted open when they raided looking for ganja and criminals.

HEAVEN was a place with a most beautiful view of Kingston Harbour.

If they caught an intruder in HEAVEN, the residents might sometimes strip them naked and force them to walk back down the rocky pathways to 'civilization' on the main Windward Road and public embarrassment.

But if you were a welcome guest in HEAVEN, you could sit and smoke a fragrant spliff and listen to the long-time residents and elders of Rastafari discuss life, the world, and the greatness of God, JAH RASTAFARI.

The "criminals" of HEAVEN were what one friend of mine called "the rebel slaves of an unjust society" – men whose alternative to starvation was robbery and violence – the only means of livelihood for those who found themselves adults and near-adults in a society in which they were not equipped to earn a living, except as manual labourers – an occupation with greater supply than demand in the Jamaican ex-slave colony.

The "criminals" of HEAVEN could be identified by the sweet harmonies they produced when gathered around a guitar in a hymn of praise to Zion – harmonies perfected in the many years of confinement in the Hell of the General Penitentiary, Kingston, where they served lengthy and unjust sentences for smoking, possessing and selling the Holy Wisdom Herb (decreed a crime), or for releasing their anger and frustrations in acts of robbery or violence.

It was in HEAVEN that I first learned about the equality of man, the possibility of a world in which each received according to their needs, gave according to their ability, and lived in love with their fellow men and women. The residents of HEAVEN called this philosophy "COMMUNAL-ism" and said it came from Africa.

On moonlight nights when the shacks and houses of HEAVEN's hillside were clearly outlined, the residents would be lulled to sleep by the rhythms and harmonies of Nyabinghi Rastafari singing and drumming coming from Count's Essie's yard nearby. In the peace and love which filled the entire hillside community, men hiding in the hills from police arrest would creep gently down through the macca bushes and gather in the dark of mango trees to add their sweet harmonic voices to the concert of praise to the Creator, JAH.

    We sat on stools among some men sitting in the shade of a zinc shelter at the back of Brother Dougie's house. He built me a spliff and as I lit it, Tommy McCook took up his saxophone and began to blow some of the sweetest music I had ever heard. The men around me smiled and made happy noises, one picked up an empty cooking pot and began beating a rhythm on the bottom, two others began to sing in harmony.

    Thereupon began the happiest days of my life. Here, with the dirt of Brother Dougie's yard under my expensive London shoes, with the smoke of the wood fire mixing with the smoke of ganja spliffs and chillum pipes being puffed by strange-looking men sitting all around me, I began my growing up as a Rasta.

    I was so happy, I was smiling and smiling and smiling. Being in that backyard, so far away from everything and anything I had ever experienced in my life before, was simply the most wonderful experience of my entire life. It was a wonderful re-birth, the start of a new life in a Jamaica I had never known before, never even knew existed.

I was truly born again right there in 1972 in Dougie Mack's yard, a completely new person, given a chance to live my life all over again. A door had opened into a new world, and I was so very glad to be entering it, like an explorer finding a new civilization on a new planet. Brother Dougie's home became the fountain of my knowledge, my education, and my development into the person I am today.

HEAVEN!
What sweet memories!
THANK YOU DOUGIE MACK!!!

RASTAFARI ROOTZFEST - A SHINING EXAMPLE OF RASTAFARI UNITY

Published online - 2015

Behold how good and how pleasant it is for brethren to dwell together in UNITY. PSALM 133

This Psalm was brought to life in 2015 at the Rastafari RootzFest-HIGH TIMES Cannabis Cup held in Negril November 12-15, 2016. The event was a celebration of joy for the changes in the Dangerous Drugs Act that decriminalized ganja for medical purposes, with some freedoms allowed to Jamaican individuals to grow and carry small amounts, as well as recognition of Rastafari Sacramental Rights, by all those whose daily lives had been conducted under the fear of arrest for partaking of a plant. The thousands of Rastas who have passed on to higher heights before seeing the fulfillment of their life campaign, must have been looking down and smiling with the same joy being expressed by the thousands gathered at the beautiful Negril Beach Park that weekend.

Most of all, Rastafari RootzFest was a celebration of RASTA Unity that many people claim no longer exists within the movement at home. The disputes that had taken center stage were nowhere in sight, as Rastafari Brethren, Sisters and children from all Mansions joined together in UNITY to participate in the event and show their approval of the revision of Jamaica s Dangerous Drugs Law. All the Mansions Nyhabinghi, Twelve Tribes, Boboshanti, House of Dread, School of Vision, Youth Initiative Council, as well as ganja farmers representing several Parishes united in Negril in a show of solidarity that surely signaled a new beginning for Rastafari under the opportunities and freedoms of the renewed law.

US magazine *HIGH TIMES*, an outspoken advocate of legalization for recreational use, partnered with a group of Rastafari to hold the first Cannabis Cup Jamaica as a major feature of Rootzfest and there was some doubt about this unusual partnership. But *HIGH TIMES* did not impose and it was clear that this was truly a RASTA event. People eagerly anticipated the event as an opportunity to earn at the booth they had rented in the Rasta Cultural Village, and especially of how eagerly they were looking forward to an event that allowed them to use ganja as freely as they desired.

The Long Bay Beach Park is a mile-long stretch of the beautiful white sand Negril beach that has been set aside for the public. On one side of the land a vast football field held tents displaying samples and promotional material of ganja products from Jamaican and US entrepreneurs, as well as samples and buds of ganja. These booths attracted the most interest from the many foreigners present happy to buy good ganja legally for the first time, visiting the stalls and learning more about exotic strains and new products such as BHO a.k.a 'shatter', a THC extract turned into a dry gum or oil that is the new and healthier way of using ganja through electronic smokeless vaporizer pipes.

. The other half of the Park housed the Rastafari Cultural Village the real heart of the festival and a beautiful scene of RASTA life. First a food court with several stalls offering a variety of Ital dishes, then a cluster of tents housing Rastafari Mansions - Nyahbinghi, Twelve Tribes, House of Dread, School of Vision, Boboshanti leading into a beautiful craft exposition spread out under trees on the sand.

Tents fluttered Red, Gold and Green decor and pictures of the Emperor. There was jewelry of all kinds from a variety of natural woods, seeds and beads; steam chalices with short and long pipes; intricately carved calabash bowls; fresh fruit and squeezed juices. But most of all, most stalls offered branches and buds of ganja for sale, as well as products made from ganja such as oils for medicine, foods, cosmetics and wines. Tent holders seemed happy with the flow of business and music gave appropriate sounds for the occasion.

On Saturday the sunshine welcomed a crowd of visitors to the Village. At midday Priest Fagan of the Rastafari School of Vision conducted Sabbath prayers, then music by Natural High sound system provided an Irie backdrop to the comings and goings of the curious and the committed. As dusk fell at Sabbath close, Ras Iv-I led a Nyabinghi chant that gathered a large crowd of participants, singing and dancing to the drumbeat. Short speeches closed the ceremony, and the Village settled in to receive the night s visitors.

On the beach, the crowd gathered by a Sumfest-level stage featuring a dynamic opening performance by Jah9, who showed why she is in such international demand. Performances followed by Luciano, The Mighty Diamonds and I-Wayne. I couldn't help thinking of all the GanJAH warriors who fought the hard battle to get Jamaica to this day when the herb is FREE to use GanJAH warriors now ancestors whose spirits were surely with us in Negril.

Special mention must be made of five people whose work was crucial to the event's success.

Ras Iyah-V was statesman-like in his speeches and presentations. He is to be commended for being bold enough to accept the HIGH TIMES proposal, despite much negative pressure, and to make it manifest in a manner that was both sacramental as well as economic. His constant insistence that grass roots ganja farmers must be the chief beneficiaries of the revised law, gives confidence that he will use the power and influence that the success of the RootzFest has given him to keep that objective in sight.

- Professor Charles Nesson shocked his Harvard University Law School years ago when he admitted being a ganja smoker. Through his love of Jamaica, he followed the discussions leading to the revised ganja law, then persuaded his HIGH TIMES friends to partner with Rastafari In Inity to celebrate the new GanJAH Freedoms. Nesson s activism at the highest levels of the national and international legalization campaign provided the assurance the organizers needed to move forward with the project. His presence at the event (with his wife Fern, whose photos decorate this article) added to the organizational help.

- Sister Mitzie Williams is well known as a RASTA voice on many issues and actions. At RootzFest her quiet supervision of all aspects of the event, and her motherly female personality provided the confidence and firm foundation on which the event proceeded.

Rick Cusick, *HIGH TIMES* Editor deserves praise for the easy manner in which he manifested the partnership with RASTA culture. *HIGH TIMES* funding and the contacts that brought so many foreign exhibitors to compete joyously in Jamaica, enabled the event to be an excellent start for what has now become a regular annual event. Many eyes were opened by the Cannabis Cup and it was good to see Jamaican entries among the winners.

- And last, but by no means least, the then-Minister of Justice Senator Mark Golding who deserves the highest commendation and praise from the Rastafari community for the measured and intelligent way in which he guided the revision of the ganja laws through Parliament, with especial consideration for the Rastafari community. Ignoring critics, Golding treated the RASTA community with total RASpect throughout the process and has thereby earned himself in return a similar high level of RASpect and LOVE.

. Rastafari RootzFest 2015 was a very peaceful 4 days and nights of Rastafari UNITY, with not a single incident of crime, no fights, not even a bag snatching.

Some of the celebrities who mingled with the crowd included Rohan Marley, Donisha Prendergast, Jah9, Chronnix, Kiddus I, Jah Cure and Mutabaruka. It was wonderful to have been there and I look forward to a bigger, better event at its 4th staging this December 14-16, 2018.

REPORT ON THE MISSION TO AFRICA REPORT

(First published August 29, 2010 after a Seminar held at UWI on the 1960 Rastafari Mission Report written by MG Smith, Rex Nettleford and Roy Augier)

The Mission to Africa was the most important step ever taken by the Jamaican Government to try to find a way to either integrate the Rastafari believers into the society, or provide a way to effect the return to Africa of those who desired repatriation. Nine persons were selected for the delegation, including three Rastafari representatives: Filmore Alvaranga, Douglas Mack, Sam Clayton and Mortimo Planno. Two reports were submitted, one of which is discussed here after its presentation to a Seminar organized by RasTafari members of the UWI faculty and the wider RasTafari community.

Before writing a report on the 2010 UWI Rasta Studies Conference, I decided to take time to read the Report which the UWI said had formed the basis of, and reason for, the conference. I am glad I did, because what I read within the pages shocked me and caused me to question not only the reason and reality of the conference, but also to state that Rastafari has been cheated, tricked, frustrated and ultimately downgraded from its founding principles, turned instead into objects of scrutiny, as unjustly imprisoned and as scorned any caged zoo animals. Brethren and Sisters, this is what I found in the document.

According to the Report, even before the first Mission to Africa set off, the authors of the document recommended that the Government of Jamaica finance the repatriation to Africa of those Jamaicans who desired it. They next recommended a mission to Africa to confirm which nations were willing to accept such emigrants, and returned with a positive invitation from all the countries visited. THAT WAS 50 YEARS AGO!

My second discovery was that one of the top recommendations was that the shacks and captured neighbourhoods where Rastafari were then living in the Western Kingston Dungle, should be converted to provide low cost housing for Rastas, as well as schools, skills training institutions, craft centers and light industries. History shows the government acted on this recommendation by bulldozing the Dungle, but when they rebuilt it became TIVOLI GARDENS with all the amenities described, but populated with supporters of the government's political party, NOT RASTAFARI. The only evidence I can see today of the intention to house Rastafari in this redevelopment, is the existence of 'Rasta City", the overgrown, abandoned corner of Tivoli Gardens made infamous during the "Dudus affair" as the burial ground for victims of assassination and murder.

My third, most important and saddest, discovery is the realization that, having authored the Report and presented recommendations 50 years ago of how to help the Rastafari nation, the UWI has not followed up by pressing succeeding governments to live up to their recommendations. Instead, the UWI has kept quiet on the injustice and betrayal, using Rastafari as subjects of continuing and continuous 'study' which has done much to elevate the reputation and scholarly degrees of several UWI personalities, but nothing whatever to advance Rastafari repatriation goals. In 50 years, during which the UWI's scholars have positioned themselves as spokespersons on such Rastafari topics as Garveyism, African history, slavery, ganja legalisation, indigenous languages AND Rastafari, not once has there been a conference, a faculty or a lecture that addressed and reinforced the very study of which the UWI is so proud.

This should have been that conference, but instead it was yet another occasion when Rastafari were placed behind the zoo bars again – the only exception being that some of those outside the bars commenting on the animals inside were some of the animals themselves, proud of their position outside the cage with a microphone in their hands.

Rastafari are not to be blamed. Most, like I, have never read the Report, so could not know the extent to which Rastafari have been betrayed. Some rare voices, like Bro. Sam Clayton, would always speak emphatically about 'the Report' and say how clearly all the visited nations endorsed Repatriation by African-descended Jamaicans, urging anyone who would listen to help make repatriation a reality. But generally I&I knew little of the recommendations, while we got to know so much more about the authors of the report, who grew in power and influence with the growth and global influence of the cultural phenomenon which they had been appointed to observe.

Rex Nettleford, who was at the time of the Report a mere Lecturer in Government, went on to become the most powerful man in Jamaica, sitting on the boards of every major Jamaican corporation of commerce and industry and appointed to every important government agency of education and culture. The 'king', as he was known, was also a king-maker, who influenced the appointments of senior executives, cultural and political

Through Red, Gold & Green Spectacles   43

leaders in every sector of the island during his lifetime. So powerful was he, that ever since he died in February there has been a link to photos of his funeral ceremony on the GLEANER's online homepage – a privilege not accorded to the recent funerals of such luminaries as former Prime Minister Hugh Shearer and Lady Gladys Bustamante.

Yet, though his links with the Afrocentric/Pan-African/Rastafari movement afforded him a rapid rise from the ranks of mere governance to an international reputation as a champion of African culture, I cannot recall the professor ever once using this enormous power and influence to remind his powerful connections of the calls for Rastafari repatriation and the recommendations of which he was one of three authors.

Professor Barry Chevannes, whose studies of Rastafari began in the 70s as a guitar-playing singer, who converted his cultural interest into 'scholarly research' and an eventual doctorate and leadership of the UWI 'Rastafari studies' movement, (*now deceased but alive when this was written*) has inherited Rex's now-vacant 'throne' as the head of the UWI's 'Rasta-centric' professors and is also heading both the government's Parliamentary commissions on Ganja reform AND reparations. With keynote speaker Sir Roy Augier now 83 and the only surviving author of the Report, Chevannes was the de facto conference head. The role of the other UWI professors will be described later.

It is shocking to see the total disregard with which those who should, have not acted on the recommendations of the 50-year old Report. Looking at the fact that Chevannes recommendations on Ganja reform have not been acted on in 10 years since they were presented, and realizing how cleverly the issues of the 50-year Report have been buried by a long line of UWI academics and admirers, one cannot help but agree with the pessimists (including Professor Augier) who think there will be similar lack of success for the now-stalled Reparations Commission's recommendations. But I digress.

WHAT THE REPORT SAYS

The report first gives a quite clear history of the Rastafari movement and what Rastafari believe. It begins by saying why and how the three authors were called together to write a Report It says that the commencement of large-scale emigration to Britain, the decline of revivalism and the activities of political parties helped the Rastafari movement grow rapidly. It explains the political mindset of the urban and rural poor, for whom Bedward and Garvey were important influences, and explains how these two were followed by Howell, Hibbert and Dunkley, explaining how each explained and lived the doctrine. There is also some history of encounters with police.

By the way, THERE IS NO MENTION OF REPARATIONS whatsoever within its pages. This shows me that the dominant word at the time the Report was written was REPATRIATION, and that at no time in the visits to Africa was there a discourse among Rastafari to finance Repatriation by Reparations. The word simply does not appear in any of the reports, or in the entire document. (Surprised!? Me too! Sir Roy Augier advised the Rastafari at the Opening Ceremony to consider remaining in Jamaica, saying of reparations: "***It nah go happen. Nah go happen. (It's not going to happen.)***" As someone knighted by the Queen of England, he should know.

FOCUS ON HOWELL & PINNACLE

Of special focus is the history of Leonard Howell and of Pinnacle, giving a clear description of it. We all know the history of how Howell's teachings were considered subversive by the establishment, and that it was at Pinnacle that Nyahbinghi flowered with strength. What I hardly knew was that the Nyahbinghi Order was considered the most threatening and subversive of Rastafari groups because of the preaching "Death to Black and White oppressors".

While I had thought that the Nyahbinghi Order was the first and foundation Rasta Mansion, the Report describes several other Rasta Mansions and groups set up by such leaders as Hibbert, Dunkley, Planno and others, plus the EWF, but the large Nyahbinghi Order of followers of founder Howell is specially described as 'violent'. The account even describes the residents of Pinnacle as praedial thieves who terrorised the rural farmers living around the property and raided their crops. The Report says that members of the Nyahbinghi Order were committed to a violent overthrow of 'Babylon', reporting:

"According to an account in The Times, the Ethiopian Emperor was head of the Niahbinghi Order, the purpose of which was the overthrow of white domination by racial war. The criminal commitment to violence and disorder reinforced the Nyahbinghi doctrine of: 'Death to white oppressors and their black allies.' Anti-social behaviour became a positive goal for some and a mark of pride for others .... This violent note had already been struck by Howell .... and the Nyahbinghi commitment to racial violence generalized the violence already preached by Howell."

The Report states that Howell was discredited by his followers for declaring himself God and his support dwindled. After Howell's Pinnacle was finally destroyed by the police, the number of locksmen increased and also bad blood increased between brethren and police. "The breakup of Pinnacle was linked with the sudden appearance of marching bands of locksmen in Kingston. The police ... may have assumed that these ...were of Howell's persuasion and were quick to act before trouble broke out."

Many Brethren – whether Nyahbinghi or not — were imprisoned, beaten, had their locks cut. Actions like these caused great confrontations between Rastafari and police, but it was clear that there was some sympathy for Rastafari among the poor, creating a danger of civil unrest. The Report was a means by Government to find answers to an obvious problem. They asked Sir Arthur Lewis, then head of the UCWI, to recommend 3 qualified persons to conduct a study, and the Report is what was delivered to Government.

RECOMMENDATIONS

Under the heading '*WHAT RASTAFARI BRETHREN WANT*' the Report states: Though the movement recognizes no single leader, common desires can be found. Most important of this is: THE RASTAFARI BRETHREN ALL WANT REPATRIATION. This is top of the list. It is backed up by a survey the writers did, in which all whom they spoke to said they wanted repatriation. The report continues:

"We are strongly of the opinion that the Government of Jamaica should take the initiative in arranging for the emigration to Africa and settlement therein of Jamaicans who wish to go there. Emigration is necessary, and the government has a duty to discover whether it is possible and to exploit every possibility."

This was stated years ago!!! Not one thing has been done to fulfill this recommendation!!!

The report gives as reasons for their recommendations: *"While many Rastafari brethren would stay in Jamaica if they found work and good social conditions, a large number have religious and emotional ties with Africa that cannot be destroyed."*

The Report also states that Jamaica is overpopulated and cannot find work for its citizens, but that "*...emigration to Africa will not be possible unless the Jamaican government takes certain initiatives.*" Nothing whatsoever has been done about this. Not one thing!!!

Speaking at the conference Opening Ceremony, Sir Roy Augier said he believed the reasons why none of the main recommendations had been acted on was "politics". The government of Norman Manley that commissioned it changed to a Bustamante-led JLP one, and no government since has bothered to follow up.

Sir Roy Augier is a distinguished academic, so intellectually and socially qualified that he has been knighted by the Queen of England. Nettleford was a winner of the Cecil Rhodes scholarship and an honours graduate of England's Oxford

University, whose clipped Oxonian speech identified him as a perfect Black Englishman – the right example (supported by the Anglicised Manley family) for citizens unwilling to unshackle their minds from the mental slavery of colonialism. The academic origins of both men show their motivation to maintain the status quo that sustained and maintained them.

However, the conference was organised and supervised by some notable UWI Rastafari academics including Rastas who should have been leading the charge against the lack of action on the Report. Professor Jalani Niah, Dr. Michael Barnett, Dr. K'adamawe K'nife and graduate Bobo Arthur Newland all had leadership roles in structuring the conference. Also present was former Folk Philosopher, Jerry Small, so I am surprised that none of them tried to focus the conference on the Report and its important revelations for Rastafari.

I keep hearing Bongo Daniel and Bongo Shefan's voices booming through the conference on several occasions: **"We want to go home!"** I can see why they are so angry. They have been waiting 50 years on the recommendations of the Report to be fulfilled. I, whose Rasta trod began 20 years after the Report was written, didn't even know its contents and recommendations!!!! How many more Rastas didn't know either?

OTHER RECOMMENDATIONS MADE 50 YEARS AGO!!!!

The Government of Jamaica should send a mission to African countries to arrange for immigration of Jamaicans. Representatives of Rastafari should be included in the Mission. (Accomplished)

The police should ... cease to persecute peaceful Rastafari brethren.

The building of low rent houses should be accelerated and provision made for self-help co-operative building.

Government should acquire the principal areas where squatting is taking place and arrange for water, light, sewerage disposal and collection of rubbish.

Civic centers should be built with facilities for technical classes, youth clubs, child clinics. The churches and the UCWI should collaborate.

The Ethiopian Orthodox Church should be invited to establish a branch in West Kingston. (Accomplished)

Rastafari brethren should be assist|ed to establish co-operative workshops.

Press and radio facilities should be accorded to leading members of the movement. (Is Muta's weekly radio show enough?). The Report also states: *"As for ganja, all experience shows that this trade cannot be stopped by trying to catch the individual smoker."*

WHAT SHOULD BE DONE?

We cannot allow the wool to be pulled over our eyes again. Prof. Jalani speaks about having Rasta conferences every 3 years. Who wants to still be here then? Why should we be encouraged to remain in Jamaica as subjects of research, rather than living in Africa as residents of I&I own home, which is I&I only and original desire? Would the many scholars and supporters of Rastafari find I&I less interesting if they interviewed and filmed us in Africa? I don't think so. In fact, I think that after 50 years, its time we moved on. To Africa. There can be no true Rasta who is not fulfilling his African dream.

Now that the Report has been published twice in I&I lifetime, we must take action by ourselves now, as we have been made stronger by the musical and intellectual growth of Rastafari in this half century all over the world. We have friends who will support us.

It is time for I&I to take some diplomatic and political steps to bring the recommendations of the Report to the attention of the present Government and also the public so that action can finally be taken. I hope others agree, and if so, I invite suggestions.

We cannot and must not let this pass without comment and action.

THE EMANCIPATION PARK STATUE

2019

I recently had cause to remember my personal Emancipation Park experience when Kanye West was allowed to hold a great, historic, free gospel concert there and some people objected, speaking about the Park as if it was some kind of hallowed ground blessed by the blood of our slave ancestors whose lives are commemorated there. Foolish protest, especially with the history of the Emancipation Park statues.

The Emancipation Park monument features two naked Africans who look like they are waiting on the block to be sold as slaves, their bodies and sexual organs visible for buyers to judge the value of the human livestock. They are not celebrating Emancipation, they look more like they are mourning.

The statue was officially designed as a national monument to represent the struggle for the Emancipation of Jamaica's

Through Red, Gold & Green Spectacles 55

enslaved Africans. So they say. Renowned Jamaican sculptor Laura Facey won the design competition to create the monument.

From its unveiling, the prominent male genitals have been controversial. But the original design for the Emancipation Park statues did not feature a large penis. The figures in original illustration ended just below the waist, the rest of the bodies were to be submerged in water. How the genitals grew from the design to the reality is a story whose details are never revealed, though rumor has a version.

Since its unveiling in July 2003, no Emancipation Day event, or national event of any kind, has been held in the space beside or around the Emancipation Statue. Since its unveiling in 2003, no politicians, no State Visitor, no VIP or special overseas guest has been photographed laying a wreath at the foot of the statues commemorating the end of slavery. Instead, the corner on which the statues stand, has become a place for public anti-government demonstrations, a popular LGBT meeting place and, at night, location of petty crimes, fights and thefts.

The invitation to the 2013 Opening of Emancipation Park took place several months before the statue was installed, and featured a picture of the design in which the two bodies end a little below the navel, with no visible genitalia. I still have a copy of the Invitation, because I had some involvement with the Emancipation Statue.

In 2012 I lived in a five-storey apartment block on Oxford Road. It was a lovely location. Our southern view from the third floor was of the downtown city with a glimpse of the sea, while on our northern side we had a view of the mountains overlooking the New Kingston business district on the corner of Oxford Road and Knutsford Boulevard, and of the large open space that used to be the Liguanea Golf Course that was in the process of being landscaped to become Emancipation Park.

Working at home writing articles for the Sunday HERALD paper, I had a good view of the construction going on, so I watched the development. Government had promised that a new and well-designed Emancipation Park to honour Jamaican history would be created for public use out of land which had once been accessed only by wealthy elite playing golf, a much-needed facelift for the city's main intersection, and Jamaicans were invited to submit designs for an Emancipation Statue to be the central monument.

Noting the invitation, I was inspired one day to use my artistic skills and draw a design for the monument. I thought about what Emancipation meant and how to translate it into a monument design. To me, Emancipation was a struggle for freedom won. No more hard work without pay for someone else, no more using my hands to feed someone other than my family.

The image of hands came to me vividly. I saw a hand reaching up towards the sky, towards freedom – a hand free of chains.

I had a friend whose craft was making stained glass who did some beautiful work, a small butterfly to hang in a window, or a set of massive entrance doors depicting an underwater scene for a wealthy client's mansion. I was always impressed with how beautiful light looks through coloured glass. I thought it would be nice to have a monument featuring a bright sun of stained glass and a hand reaching up to that sun, through whose rays flow streams of light reflecting the colors of the sun and the sky, the light of a new Jamaican day of freedom.

I saw the hand reaching up to stars made of aluminum mined from our Jamaican earth, and the names of our Emancipation Heroes etched on the stars, with spaces to add a new star with another Hero's name every Emancipation Day in a special Ceremony at the Statue.

I was very proud as I drew my design, made a finished copy and wrote words describing what it depicted. It wasn't easy to fulfill the competition specifications for mounting my entry, which instructed that designs should be submitted on paper measuring 2 feet by 3 feet. I bought the paper, made a cardboard protective cover and set off to deliver my entry by bus to the designated address at the Jamaica National Heritage Trust offices at Duke Street. It wasn't easy to get my package up the bus steps, but there were few passengers on board, so I took a double seat and enjoyed the ride with my cardboard companion all the way downtown.

Arriving finally at Tower Street, I walked one block west to Headquarters House, the 19th Century mansion used as the seat of Jamaica's Parliament until the 1960s when the new Parliament at Gordon House was built. Nowadays the historic building was the headquarters of the Jamaica National Heritage Trust, the concierge of Jamaica's historical treasures of land, buildings, artefacts and historic sites. It was here that entries for the Emancipation monument should be delivered.

A young lady came out and attended to me. She took charge of the large package, brought a book for me to sign with my name and address, and took away my entry. I went back home, satisfied that I had delivered my entry in the competition.

I continued watching the daily development of the Park from upstairs in my apartment and waited to hear the results of the competition. It was fascinating to watch the land being transformed into a national project of which all Jamaica would be proud. We were told that the ironwork around the park would feature African symbols, that there would be a paved running track, a stage, a children's play area, a fountain, lots of green grass.

And there would be a monument to honour and represent Emancipation.

Results were announced and my design was not the winner. The competition had been won by Laura Facey, a great sculptor some of whose most beautiful work I had seen in the University of Technology's Statue Park. She is certainly one of Jamaica's best artists, and a lovely person as well.

I didn't think much of the winning design though. It featured two naked bodies, a man and a woman, looking up to the sky with serious faces. The bodies were cut off at navel height and seemed to be standing in what was explained to be water or earth.

The design didn't make me feel like Emancipation. I didn't like the nakedness of the human bodies. I felt the first thing freed slaves would have done would have been to cover their nakedness. They should have had some sort of covering.

Why didn't the man have a machete, or even a stick in his hand to depict his labour and his fight for freedom? Why didn't the woman have a child with her, one of her children? Were they not a family? I didn't see anything in the statues that showed the emotion that Freedom would have brought to their faces and bodies. It was just two bodies standing still, staring silently to the sky. It didn't inspire anything in me except disappointment.

It wasn't just sour grapes. I really did not think my design would have won, as I was sure there had been hundreds of other entries from some great Jamaican artists who I was sure would have submitted much better designs than I. I merely hoped the winning design would have had something more of Africa, a more revolutionary attitude, than this one did.

Ah well, no time for sour grapes, Barbara.

Someone else won, not you.

Shut up.

So I did.

I made sure I was on the invitation list for the opening. This was history. Moreover, I wouldn't need taxi fare to attend, just a brisk walk across the street. My invitation arrived, a crisp card bearing as a logo a picture of the winning entry of a man and a woman looking up. The design of the statue that was published in the newspaper, on the invitations and the programme handed out as we arrived showed the human bodies cut off just below the navel.

There were no genitals visible on either figure.

There was no sign of a male organ in the design.

There is proof in the invitations and the Program for the opening of Emancipation Park that became a keepsake.

How did that male organ happen to become part of the final statue?

One answer can be found when you follow my story of the Emancipation Statue to the end.

There was nice 4 o'clock afternoon sun as I made my way to the function in the new Emancipation Park. The ornamental trees were young, but healthy. The ornamental fence with its African symbols surrounded the large space. The running track was paved. Grass flourished on which hundreds of white chairs were laid out before the stage.

I moved to a seat near the stage, but was quickly stopped by an official who informed me that all the front seats were 'reserved for the Diplomatic Corps'. This was the first time I was really upset at the so-called protocol rule that says that every (usually White) person even at the lowest level of the diplomatic service has the right to sit in the best front row seats at every official event, even when there are Jamaicans of higher rank and importance.

I don't see why this rule exists that makes the front rows of all official events be almost exclusively rows of White people. They only ever speak to each other, occasionally graciously acknowledging the VIP politicians also seated in the front rows but not the other Jamaicans around them. I don't see why they can't sit in a special section to the left or right of the front seats, or even a special section in the middle of the seated audience, so they can sit among the people of the country to whom they have been sent to represent, while living a good life in our Jamaican paradise.

It upset me greatly to see the rows of best seats filling up with people whose skin colour showed they came from the nations from which we Jamaicans had to fight for our Emancipation. On this, of all occasions when Jamaicans would be celebrating our liberation from them, they should be sitting at the back having to strain their necks to see us freed slaves open our beautiful Emancipation Park!

JAH must have been reading my mind, because just at that moment a shower of rain fell through the sunshine, sprinkling everyone with sparkling drops. They fell on my face like the holy water the priest splashes on the congregation at the end of our Church service.

The diplomats scampered like rats.

We, the average Jamaican people accustomed to unexpected wettings as we travel by bus and on foot, just waited it out knowing it would soon be over.

It was.

Then using the little tissues or handkerchiefs we always carry to mop our sweating pedestrian brows, we average Jamaicans simply wiped off the chairs in the front rows, sat down and just stayed there. When the rain stopped the organizers tried, but realized they could not move us. They brought in dry chairs to make a new VIP row in front of us for the Prime Minister and VIPs, and then made an effort to wipe down some of the wet seats in the rows behind. The diplomats sat where they could.

So, with the help of JAH, we – the Emancipated people- got to sit up front and see the entertainment and hear the speakers expressing their tributes to the Emancipation Heroes who enabled us to be sitting there that day. An illustration of the winning Monument logo dominated the stage backdrop and showed us what we thought was to come. It was a lovely event.

Some weeks after the ceremony it was announced that there would be an exhibition of the entries in the Emancipation Statue competition to be held at the government building adjacent the Park. The announcement also informed that there were only 8 entries in the competition!

Only eight!!!

I was surprised!

HOWEVER, I was even more surprised to learn that my design was not part of the exhibition!

My entry did not exist.

It was nowhere to be found!

No one connected to the exhibition knew anything about it.

There was no record of my delivery, so carefully carried by bus, or of the JNHT receiving it.

Nothing at all.

Just when I thought I must be going crazy and that I had imagined drawing that design and taking it down to Headquarters House, I got a call from Dr. Alfred Sangster – the much-respected former Principal of the University of Technology,

"What happened to your entry in the Emancipation Park Monument competition?"

I was amazed that he knew about it, but he told me that he saw it at Headquarters House when he was one of the eminent Jamaicans who were consulted on the creation of the statue.

The way he said it made me realise he had liked my design.

I told him I had no idea what had happened to it.

Neither did he.

After that conversation, Dr. Sangster and I went down several investigative roads over quite a few years trying to find out something more about what happened to my entry. We have never found any trace of my entry, or anyone who can say anything about it.

The only information we could get about the competition was that Rex Nettleford was the competition's judge. The only judge. That's all. No one would say anything more.

It is this name that is called when people ask how come the sculptor added such a large male penis to the finished monument design, when the bodies visible in the original design on the Invitations and Programme for the Opening of the Park ended at the navel of both statues, with no genitals in sight. I was told that Nettleford, the UWI professor regarded as Jamaica's highest cultural expert, had insisted that the genitals of the male statue be not only included but generously endowed.

Whatever Rex Nettleford wanted done was always done. He was a very powerful man, especially in matters of 'culture'. The sculptor agreed to his desire and the finished statue displays an enormous male penis as prominently as the amply endowed wooden carvings on display to tourists in Fern Gully.

I wasn't the only person who didn't like the Emancipation Monument. After it was unveiled, the male penis drew a lot of controversial attention and outrage. Many said it was a national disgrace and did not represent 'Emancipation'. Many said that as descendants of those who fought for and won our Emancipation, they felt no empathy with it. The sight of male nudity offended many people's moral and religious sensibilities.

Many said the Emancipation Monument was supposed to make us think about the battles that were fought and the lives that were lost to win our freedom from enslavement by Europeans, but instead it made us think of sex and immorality. On the other hand, the male statue was greatly admired by the homosexual community, who made it a popular spot for gay men to meet and congregate at night.

I was remembering my Emancipation Monument design, as I heard the large Police presence assuring persons leaving Kanye West's concert that there was no danger that they would be mugged or robbed that night by the special breed of criminals who frequent the Statue corner of Emancipation Park.

A young and obviously gay man came up to me and begged me for 'bus fare'. He said he was 'afraid to walk home past the statue'. I gave him Two Dollars. It was all I had.

The Emancipation Park Monument is still an eyesore and source of national shame for many.

THE ISLANDER - MY LIFE IN MUSIC AND BEYOND
by Chris Blackwell   *(My BOOK REVIEW 2022)*

Chris Blackwell begins his autobiography with a story of how some Rastas once saved his life when he got lost while boating with friends in Kingston Harbour. It made me smile to read, as once when I was lost under the bitter hatred of British racism, Chris Blackwell gave me a job promoting THE HARDER THEY COME that introduced me to Rasta and saved my life. For that reason I found "The Islander – My Life In Music and Beyond" even more interesting than the average reader will.

Most readers will pick up Blackwell's book looking for juicy stories about the music celebrities with whom he has been associated from his youth, when his mother was beloved by James Bond storyteller Ian Fleming, to his adult years as the famous Island Records music producer and friend of reggae icon Bob Marley.

Yes, Blackwell calls many names in his book, but the notes he reveals are all musical. No salacious titbits about any of the many big names he calls, from Ernie Ranglin, Jimmy Cliff and Millie Small, through Stevie Winwood, Cat Stevens, U2, Grace Jones and many in between. Instead of gossip, "The Islander" is a very special handbook of the Jamaican and British music industries that all who love music will find an interesting fountain of knowledge.

JUKE BOXES AND TALENT SHOWS

Growing up as a privileged White Jamaican, Blackwell tells his story with light humour and a total lack of self-pride, revealing the details of his professional wins and losses honestly, beginning with the chance job that started him in the music business. While Chris' parents had some money, they were not so wealthy that he didn't need to work. After some tries including as aide-de-camp to the Governor General, the job he found was a hardworking slog around Jamaica's highways and by-ways installing and supplying records for a line of jukeboxes that provided musical entertainment in those days at bars and clubs.

When competition forced him to find new sources for records to replenish the jukeboxes, he decided to make his own, and with the help of record store owner Leslie Kong and Australian Graham Goodall whose band was stuck in Jamaica, he picked some singers making a name for themselves on the weekly Vere Johns talent shows, recorded them and therewith began Island Records.

From recording Jamaican artists in competition with such early producers as Duke Reid and Coxone, Blackwell expanded the Island market from Kingston to London, hoping to gain more sales from the growing Jamaican and Caribbean communities of Britain. He tells he story of bringing young Jimmy Cliff to England with the hope of making him a star (a plan that only materialized years later with Jimmy's starring role in "The Harder They Come") and finally getting lucky with Millie Small's "My Boy Lollipop" mega-hit song that finally established Island as a viable music company. Blackwell's story is fascinating because it also tells the story of the development of British music in the 'Swinging Sixties" when British music topped world charts and provided Island's inspiration and competition.

Island's success as a member of the British music industry came with his discovery of the talented young English musician Steve Winwood and the Spencer Davis Group, getting Jamaican Jackie Edwards to write songs for the group and seeing it become a successful part of the blossoming of the British 60s music scene that included the Animals, Small Faces, the Kinks, Yardbirds, Jethro Tull, the Who, and groups with names like Granny Takes A Trip and Mott the Hoople.

THE ONES THAT GOT AWAY

Blackwell signed many unknown groups and artists, explaining that Island was "always looking for the new and the next". But he tells why he didn't sign the Rolling Stones when he could, and how much he regrets passing on the group Procul

Harum that went on to record the massive hit song "A Whiter Shade of Pale", some of the episodes that make "The Islander" a fascinating read. Blackwell even admits there was a subsidiary Island label that produced X-rated albums by risqué comics like Nipsy Russell and a 'Music to Strip By" album that was sold with a G-string attached.

Reading through the detailed account of Island's music history, it is clear that Blackwell paid his dues and worked hard as a genuine member of the music industry at a time when England was the world's musical mecca, with Island turning out enough hits and hit-makers to be a serious competitor in the British and U.S. music industries. As Island grew, Blackwell gained a deep knowledge of music production and management, always relying on his instincts to select artists and artist managers to stay alive in the highly competitive industry. Music insiders and historians will enjoy the details.

Of course, what will bring most readers to the book is where Blackwell tells of how the Wailers came to his office, persuaded him to let them make an album, then went on to become one of the worlds' biggest groups ever and Bob Marley a musical icon. Most details have become well known reggae music legends. Blackwell adds more details of this very unique music history that is even more interesting because his work with the Wailers benefited from both his English links and experience, as well as the Jamaican roots that have been the foundation of his life.

One especially poignant story is about what happened at the sad end, when Bob recorded the music that was eventually released as the two albums 'Rebel Music" and "Legend". The decision to record "Redemption Song" just as an acoustic solo, also says how well Chris Blackwell knew Bob's spirit and how deeply it was expressed in that one song. Reading Blackwell's words about that part of his life and musical career, one can see the sorrow that still rests in his memory of a man who was more than just an artist, but a friend.

SLY & ROBBIE, GRACE JONES

After Bob died, Blackwell tells of "trying to fill the space Bob left behind" by building Compass Point studio in the Bahamas and bringing Sly & Robbie to join composer Willy Badarou as foundations of a studio band, hoping to offer musicians an island vibe that unfortunately could not happen in politically volatile Jamaica. His attempt to christen the studio with what he thought was a traditional Jamaican ritual of the blood of a headless chicken, led to Lee Scratch Perry's lifetime-long bad vibes, while his effort to record rock-n-roll legend James Brown there ended after 4 days. But the Rolling Stones loved Compass Point, and so did U2, the super band he signed that became Island's biggest hit group after the Wailers. Compass

Point was also where Grace Jones, the former model and disco diva, found her grove on Sly & Robbie's bass rhythms and developed into a superstar, later becoming one of Blackwell's best friends.

However, the huge success of U2 caused Island financial problems that were only solved when Blackwell sold the company to Polydor. The sad story of that episode explains a section of his life that has never before been revealed in detail. Turning his back on music after Polydor, Blackwell looked to his interest in real estate for a new career, that led to his development of a rundown beachfront section of Miami Beach into a string of world-class hotels that gave him another success story.

Despite that success, Miami could not hold him. Blackwell is truly an island boy and we Jamaicans know how the magnetic pull of our beautiful island draws us back, no matter how far we travel. The story of Blackwell's return to develop Strawberry Hill, The Caves Negril and finally Golden Eye into Jamaica's most unique celebrity hotels is told with his usual modesty in describing how, with the help of his wife Mary, he created three legendary and exclusive Jamaican resorts where he can name-drop guests like Beyonce and JayZ, Elon Musk, Prince Charles and Daniel Craig.

But no matter how famous the names may be, none have left a greater imprint on Blackwell's life than Bob Marley. As he comes to the end of his story, he admits that memories of Bob can bring tears. "Every day you hear a song, are asked questions, get sent a link to some way that Bob Marley has had an impact on the world, how he brought people of different faiths together. You realize that Marley's songs are something more than songs, and their strength keeps growing. His global reach keeps extending and it's been amazing to see that growth continue in my lifetime." he writes.

In the final chapter I realize Blackwell's book has not been written as a boast about his life achievements, but instead as a tribute to all the good friends who traveled with him along his life's way. "One way or another, I have lost many fellow travelers, friends and colleagues," he mourns in his closing words. As well as Bob, he lists actress Nathalie Delon, Millie Small, Toots Hibbert, Seeco Patterson, Sean Connery, Countryman and his great friend Dickie Jobson. His book is a loving story about them that members of the music industry – especially the Jamaican music industry, will want to read, reflect on, and learn from.

NO MORE RASTAS

(Humour) Published @ Press Reader – 2015

My dear friend Suzanne,

How nice to hear from you after all this time. Good to know you're home again after 10 years at the University of Bulgaria. Quite a change from your beloved New York!

Sure, I'd be happy to help update your thesis on Rastafari by filling you in on what's been happening in Jamaica over the past few years. You'll be very surprised at the changes!

Yes, the Rastas have all gone. There isn't a single one left in Jamaica. The anger, annoyance and irritation that Rastas brought out in so many Jamaicans, finally boiled over and became a public issue ten years ago. The people who hated Rastas became more vocal with their objections to this group of natty-headed, ganja-smoking believers in a stupid religion. All the people who used to keep their anti-Rasta opinions quiet, started writing articles and making speeches, started banning Rastas from their public places, stopped serving them in shops, and started openly boycotting anything and everything Rasta.

At first the Rastas ignored the negativity, said they were used to rejection. But the unrelenting and aggressively anti-Rasta activity forced them into confrontation and arrests by the Police.

Eventually the Rastas held a massive Nyahbinghi to discuss the situation and decided it was time to stop waiting on Reparations and just leave Jamaica. Soon after that Rastas started packing up and leaving the island. In ones, twos, in families and groups, the Rasta exodus became a daily activity.

There was major rejoicing when the Rastas left. The celebration began as a barbecue fete along a street where a large Rasta family had lived for many years, before packing everything they owned into 4 large trailers which were hauled to the wharf early one morning. The anti-Rasta women in homes on the street called each other on their cellphones and filmed the passage of the trailers past their gates. When the last one had disappeared, one woman said: Let's throw a party!

Soon it became a habit, the celebration party after Rastas departed. Downtown was partying and Uptown was rejoicing. When the last certifiable, dreadlocksed, ganja-smoking Rasta boarded a private Lear jet and flew off into the sunset, Jamaica exploded into an island-wide carnival that lasted for days and went on every weekend for weeks. For nearly a year, one could see posters for *"Dem Gone"* events of every kind stuck on billboards, light posts and in newspaper advertisements.

The *"Dem Gone"* parties all had identical features. The first rule was that no reggae music was played. Soca, Calypso, Latino, Rock & Roll, Jazz, Country & Western, Swing and even

Classical music, but not even a Lovers Rock tune. Pork was always served as the main food item, and rum was the drink of choice. Ital eating became a fad of the past, and KFC, Burger King and Wendys opened more outlets, and Island Grill changed its logo colours to green, black and gold. Clothes bore no evidence of Afrocentric designs or colours, but instead people wore clothes with only US brand names such as Versace, Dior, Hilfiger and Ralph Lauren. Nothing to remind them of the despised Rastas.

A popular talk show host started a protest against the use of Marley's *One Love* to advertise Jamaican tourism, so the JTB got Agent Sasco to record a new song *My Love* to replace it. Rasta language was banned. The UWI Department of Patois published a list of acceptable words and phrases that excluded any 'Rasta-talk' such as 'Irie' and 'Bredrin'. The JCDC re-wrote its rules, forbidding the annual Schools Dance Competitions to use music by or about Rastafari; IRIE-FM shut down, while RJR broadcast archive tapes of programmes hosted by Neville Willoughby and Don Topping.

The L'Acadco Dancers were banned as being 'too Rasta'. The NDTC cancelled its Christmas season as a mark of protest and support, while removing their dance tributes to Marley and Jimmy Cliff from their performance. The Garveyites, pleased to have a permanent break from the Rasta 'monopoly' of the philosophy of the National Hero, banned all references and associations of the name Marcus Garvey with any aspect of the Rasta movement. Textbooks were re-written accordingly.

Remedial classes were inaugurated at the Bellevue Hospital for children and adults showing any signs of interest in the Rastafari religion, such as men growing beards, girls refusing to have their hair chemically processed, or people showing an interest in African history and culture. Disdain for the British and American empires and other manifestations of colonialism and anti-Black racism was perceived as 'antisocial'.

The concerted effort has paid off and the differences of life without Rastas can be perceived. There are no more late night street dance parties pumping reggae music into the ears of sleepless neighbours, thank God. But since no one is interested in dancing the night away to the music of Frank Sinatra and Dolly Parton, people stay home and listen to the radio or watch TV instead. The nights are quiet now.

But without the calming presence of Rastafari in so many depressed communities and with the total banning of the use of ganja, the dangers of going out at night and even in the daytime in any town or city, have increased a hundred percent. There is nothing to 'ease the vibe' and make the place 'irie', as the Rasta presence used to do. Police and Army patrol the streets and ride the buses to keep things under control. They even sit in school classrooms with loaded weapons to keep off the gangs of youths who roam the streets looking for things to steal for their survival.

You see, a lot of energy has been spent on eradicating Rastafari from Jamaica, but none has been spent on improving the conditions that bred the Rasta philosophy. The poverty, deprivation, illiteracy, immorality and crime, the legacy of Jamaica's slave and colonial history that Rastafari sang and preached about and against, cannot be wiped out that easily. That would take several generations of major economic infusions to poor, unemployed and hungry people, to toally transform the communities that bred the fungus of violence.

Many people have left Jamaica because it no longer has the cultural references that made the place a cultural place to live. They moved to Atlanta or Miami or Brooklyn, where some traces of the old Jamaica still remain. Those who stayed behind in Jamaica the haves and the have-nots are locked in a permanent war without even the escape afforded by the music of Peace and Love. Jamaica has become a sad and bitter place.

No more tourists come to the beaches. They say they miss the tinkle of reggae music as they sun-tan, they say they came to meet Bob Marley and his copycats, they say they miss the language and laughing conversations with the colourful people who made Jamaica more interesting than the other islands Rastafari. They say that without the music, without that vibe,

Jamaica is no longer an interesting destination for them. The beaches in the other islands are just as pretty and the increase in Jamaica's crime has increased the dangers of their visit.

Instead they are vacationing in Africa at one of the many Rastafari settlements across the Continent. Some go to the pioneer settlement in Shashemane, Ethiopia to purchase traditional fashions, religious artefacts and Red, Gold and Green craft items. Others vacation at the Rastafari Health Spa and Hotel in Cape Town, South Africa, using it as a base for Rastafari-led safaris to African cultural destinations.

Other tourists visit the Rastafari towns and villages in Ghana, always stopping at the Boboshanti Taberbacle for blessings and healing. Some visit the music studios in Botswana where the Rastafari reggae, videos, albums and films are being made and circulated around the world via satellige, the Internet, on DVDs, CDs and tapes.

The visitors marvel at the purpose-built dwellings, orderly communities, prosperous healthy people and enviable democratic systems that Rastafari are building throughout Africa. They know these Rastafari communities have become models that are being duplicated by many African governments, bringing new ideas for African development based on Rastafari experiences and exposure in various nations, political and educational systems outside the Continent.

The visitors know also, that the wealth needed to build the Rastafari African Diaspora was provided a seven years ago by the United Nations mandate for Reparations to be paid by those European nations that had participated in and benefited from 300 years of the Transatlantic Slave Trade, making them pay for the return and resettlement in Africa of all those who wanted to leave the former slave plantations. Good people all over the world black and white rejoiced when the United Nations held negotiations that resulted in the award of Billions of US Dollars in reparations to the descendants of slavery in the African Diaspora.

The Rastas are building their African projects out of the profits earned from investing their portion of the Reparations award. As all Rasta projects in Africa so far have been profitable, the principal is still untouched.

My dear friend Suzanne, hope this short note gives you some information you can use as background for your upcoming research trip to the Rastas in Africa. I wish I could afford to come with you. To tell the truth, as a baldhead Jamaican browning, I miss them.

Look forward to reading your report.

    ONE LOVE

    Oops, sorry. Not allowed to use that phrase any more.

        Yours sincerely,

        Your friend, Elizabeth White.

JAMAICA S REGGAE FILMS - A NEW GENRE

Whether they love Roots&Culture, Reggae, Ska, Dub, Rockers, Dancehall or Lovers Rock, music lovers around the world welcome the works of film makers who have used Jamaica s music in a variety of ways that pay homage to the strength and endearing quality of its creation. Long may this trend continue.

In what some historians now refer to as the 'Rasta Reggae Seventies, films featuring Jamaica s music and culture became recognized as a new and exciting new genre and film festivals around the world began scheduling Reggae films as special features of their event s programme. Jamaica joined Hollywood, Bollywood and Nollywood as centers of a unique film genre and Jamaican film makers suddenly had ample opportunities to make and distribute their films to a global audience hungry for cinematic views of the unique culture. The enormous potential of income to be made from films depicting aspects of Jamaican culture became considered at a time when Jamaicans were being emboldened by the easy access and use of digital film making equipment to become film makers.

This all did not happen overnight. It began with Perry Henzell s 1972 movie *The Harder They Come* that became popular because it was the world's first look at the Rasta Reggae culture in which the film was set. The world sat open-mouthed watching the story set in the Kingston ghettoes where the music was born, unfold its tale of ganja and Rasta far away from the white sand tourist beaches for which Jamaica has previously been known.

THTC started an indigenous Jamaican film industry when it was made in 1972 through the herculean efforts of Perry Henzell and his team of writer Trevor Rhone and actors Jimmy Cliff, Carl Bradshaw and Ras Daniel Hartman. Several attempts were made in the 70s to follow Henzell s lead, but it took two or three more decades for that objective to be achieved, and it happened slowly and almost invisibly. Ted Bafaloukas *Rockers* the tale of ghetto reggae musicians turned Robin Hoods was the next Reggae Film, while Dickie Jobson's *'Countryman'* tapped into the image of Jamaica as an exotic haven of ganja, guns and tourists, while his brother Wayne told Peter Tosh's story in *'Stepping Razor -Red X'*. Failures like Calvin Lockhart s *'Every Ni**er Is A Star'*, and *'The Marijuana Affair'* with National Security Minister Dudley Thompson playing a police chief, did not deter the efforts.

Films mean money, so people kept making films about and with reggae, hoping to make the money that was so elusive for Henzell. Before becoming a successful politician, lawyer Laurie Broderick tried his hand at film production with the dancehall feature film *Kla$h* starring Black American stars Jasmine Guy and Giancarlo Esposito, with Jamaican actor Carl Bradshaw. Having tasted success with his *The Harder They Come* music partnership, record mogul Chris Blackwell established Palm Pictures that produced 3 Jamaican films including *The Lunatic, Dancehall Queen* and *Third World Cop* - the most financially successful and longest-running Jamaican film ever. But somehow the efforts attracted little international attention or distribution.

Film making was not restricted to Jamaicans. The plum film making prize for many Jamaicans was a job on a foreign feature film, beginning with productions in the 1960s including *Doctor No* (1962) with Sean Connery and Ursula Andress, and *A High Wind In Jamaica* (1964) starring Anthony Quinn and James Coburn. In the 1980s a flock of foreign films used Jamaica as a scenic backdrop, including *Club Paradise* with Robin Williams, Peter O Toole and Jimmy Cliff, *Cocktail* with Tom Cruise, *Clara's Heart* with Whoopie Goldberg and *The Mighty Quinn* starring Denzel Washington. Impressive names, and a lot of good work done promoting Jamaica s vacation paradise, but nothing that gave a feeling of full pride in describing a Jamaican film industry.

In 2007 Peter Gittins, an English reggae and film enthusiast and archivist, wrote asking if he could include my documentary film *Race, Rhetoric, Rastafari*, produced for CHANNEL FOUR-UK, in a database collection of 'Reggae Films'. I was surprised to learn there was such a genre of films, but he informed that Jamaica's reggae music had influenced a lot of film makers to documents aspects of the culture and people who made it. His contact inspired the launch of an annual series of Reggae Film Festivals from 2008 to 2013 showcasing the films and Jamaican culture.

Under the umbrella of the Ministry of Culture s first Reggae Month and with the help of several sponsors, Peter Gittins and I organized the first Reggae Film Festival which took place at Emancipation Park under a full moon eclipse on February 22, 2008, followed by two more nights of films at the Island Auditorium in New Kingston. It was a huge success. The impact of the Reggae Film Festival went beyond the event s success and the good vibe it generated in the local film industry. News of the Festival travelled to all the countries where blogs, websites and magazines on reggae picked up the story, publishing articles about the films and film makers, and developing interest in Jamaican film making.

The Reggae Film Festival continued for 8 years, generating growing attention to films about reggae. Films about Reggae events in Africa, Israel, Serbia, to name a few, Ska concerts that keep that genre alive, feature films from South

America, Germany, Norway, were just a few of the works screened.

Almost overnight, the world woke up to the fact that Jamaica s reggae music has inspired a new genre of films that have earned their own classification. For 8 years I was able to present three or four nights of films about reggae artists, reggae genres and films with reggae soundtracks made by film makers from all over the world. The film makers may not have been born here, but what has inspired them has been the heartbeat music of Jamaica s reggae music the unique sound that the little island of 3 million people produced, and continues to produce.

Sadly, after trying to do it by myself, the Reggae Film Festival didn't get the financial support it needed for success. I know I should have just handed it over to the Government, but I didn't see a commitment that I felt was necessary to keep the event tied to its Rastafari roots, or to keeping me in charge of it. It was my 'baby' and I didn't want to hand it over to strangers, so I continued on my own, making a positive contribution to film in Jamaica, if not my pocket.

In the years since the first Reggae Film Festival, several Reggae films have been completed or are in production, and many have been welcomed by the Reggae film circuit.

Best of all have been the many opportunities the RFF gave for Jamaican film makers to expose their talent for the first time to a Jamaican audience. One offshoot has been the development of a Jamaican animated film industry led by Kevin Jackson, with great work by Ricardo *Mental* Chung.

Everything changed positively as technology developed digital film production. The need for music videos to promote the prolific reggae music industry led to the development of a small cadre of music videographers led by Ras Kassa, Jay Will and Nordia Rose whose works could be classified as award-worthy mini-movies displaying creativity and competence.

This inspired exciting new Jamaican feature films that showed a fresh approach to storytelling and film making. Inspired by them, a new breed of young film makers armed with digital cameras and computer editing suites emerged onto the film landscape, led by Storm Saulter.

Sadly, lack of economic support caused Peter and me to end our patriotic effort in 2013 and since then we have noticed that the number of reggae films has declined. While it lasted, the Reggae Film Festival produced an archive of nearly 300 reggae films of all kinds, biographies of reggae artists and producers, films with reggae soundtracks, and films of reggae events around the world. I am still trying to have this collection of films established at a location where they can be used for screenings and for research by persons interested in this aspect of Jamaican culture.

While we all hope for a flourishing of Jamaican creative art in film, especially films for the Jamaican Diaspora, the global trend for Rasta Reggae culture provides a sure means of reaching the lovers of film in countries around the world. I can only hope the trend continues, especially the recording of the history of reggae on film for our archives and our children. I would like to see an annual fund established for recording more of the history of reggae. We need films about artists like Lee 'Scratch' Perry, Toots Hibbert, Sly & Robbie and those behind-the-scenes personalities like the founders of the original, historic Reggae Sunsplash, MC/Producer Tommy Cowan and the female harmony trio I-Three that backed Bob Marley.

I look forward to that hope becoming a reality.

- - -

TELL ME SOMETHING GOOD

('Powerful Men & Women Perform for Charity' - Comedy show - 2017)

GOOD EVENING EVERYONE! NICE TO SEE YOU ALL!

My friend Bob Marley came to visit me the other night in a dream. I haven't seen Bob for 37 years, so it was good to have a chat with mi old friend.

What you doing here, I ask him.

Bob smile and say:

I jus' a-tek a look pon the Gideon. I see say the earth still a-run.
What a-gwan?

Me tell him: Nuff t'ings a-gwan, mi Lion. Nuff nuff. What you wan' hear 'bout?

Bob say to me:

Tell me something Good, mi Sista. Give me some Good News.
Tell me something good about CLIMATE CHANGE.

Tell me say the climate stop change because everybody stop doing the things that were makin' it change.

Tell me say them stop burn fossil fuels; tell me say them solve the Fukishima problem, and tell me say people learn to recycle plastic.
That a-gwan?

I had to tell him: Not yet, Bob.
So Bob say to me:

Well tell me something good about RACISM.
Tell me that everybody realize that we are all one Human Race, with lots of different-different people just like how there are different-different flowers and fruits and them t'ings, but everybody is just same One People.

Tell me say we now have a different kind of RACE-ism, everybody working for the Human Race.

I had to tell him: Not yet Bob. Racism still dey 'bout everywhere.
Bob say:
So that sound like you still have WAR down there.
You people don't stop that yet?
WARmongers still using WAR to get power over people?

I had to tell him we still got WAR down here. Too much.
Bob neva like that.
Him say:

If you still have WAR, that means you still have MONEY down there.
Tell me something GOOD about money. Tell me that the people with all the MONEY sharing it out equally among everybody
Tell me say they realize MONEY no longer important.
Tell me something GOOD about MONEY.

But I had to tell Bob there was nothing good to tell him about MONEY.
Still causing strife and hate and greed and poverty.
Bob think a little. Then him tell me to tell him something GOOD about HUNGER.
Like how crops are plentiful and nobody is hungry any more.

But when I tell him NO, him get angry.

How you mean you still have HUNGER? What all you people down there doing?
Just fighting WAR and changing the climate and hating each other's RACE??

What a-gwan???

I tell Bob I am doing my best to change things, but is only a few of us.

So Bob say:

Tell me something GOOD about FAMILY, that FAMILY has become the most important unit of society. That everyone finally realized that Father, Mother and Children is the most valuable group for building a nation.

Tell me say all the countries in the world have Family Life as the most important Ministry of every Government.

But I tell him that Sad to say, Beloved Brother, this is not so. The example of the Holy Father, Holy Mother and Holy Son is lost to many. Families are still broken, children still grow up without a parent or two, many still suffer abuse, cruelty, poverty and lack of education. Can't tell you something GOOD about FAMILY today!

So Bob think a little more, then him say:

Well tell me something GOOD about LOVE.

Tell me say people on Earth finally know LOVE.

I was really glad to tell Bob that LOVE is one thing I can tell him something GOOD about.

I tell him say his song ONE LOVE did a lot to make people realise that is only LOVE that can the world be 'alright', that we have to LOVE one another and live in LOVE.

I tell him say his song influenced the whole world.

I tell him say him message gone abroad!

I tell him say people sing ONE LOVE every day, everywhere in the world, in every language, in every country.

I tell him say him song mek the whole world a-talk about LOVE and nuff people trying to live in LOVE.

But Bob stop me right there and say:

Is not MY message Barbara.

Is the message of Christ, that LOVE is the greatest Commandment.

I can't tek no credit or no royalties for that message, Sis.

Is Christ did say that to LOVE is to be God, for GOD IS LOVE.

Me just repeat him words inna Reggae style like Selassie taught me.

Bob say:
LOVE is the only way to change all the things me just speak about.
Because if we LOVE the Planet like how we LOVE weself and if we love oneanother, all these problems will be solved.
LOVE is the answer.
That's what we need more of.
LOVE.

Me say me agree with him.
Bob smile.

Well me glad to hear the song a-gwan good.
And me glad that the one thing you can tell me something GOOD about is LOVE.
Gwan keep the faith, mi Sister.
PEACE and ONE LOVE.

As Bob say that, I hear some ONE LOVE music start to play, 'ONE LOVE, ONE HEART, Let's get together and feel alright."

And jus' as me start to dance, Bob just fly 'way back home.

Me did glad fi see him.

Him gone, but I glad say him music don't gone nowhere.

Bob lef' him music to keep us happy and remind us of JAH LOVE.

Thank you Bob.
ONE PERFECT LOVE

RASTAFARI - JAMAICA'S NEXT NATIONAL HERO

In my humble opinion, it's RASTAFARI, not just Bob Marley, that should be declared Jamaica's next National Hero.

I admit that I have been one of the many calling for Marley to be declared a National Hero, and the call has grown louder since Barbados elevated a singing star to that status as it became a Republic. But in seriously considering whether Bob qualifies for National Hero status, I have to evaluate whether in becoming a global musical superstar and multimillionaire, Bob Marley has done any of the things that have earned him the right to be remembered for ever in that elevated category, more than the national decorations he already has.

First, let us consider what it is that has earned our present Heroes their titles. In so doing, it is clear that each one, in a special and individual way, has fought and won a battle that took Jamaica from one status to a higher level. Let us examine each.

Paul Bogle and George William Gordon were sacrificed in the early battle to emancipate Jamaica from slavery and colonialism, and their battle ended with their deaths. No one can deny their right to be elevated to Hero status. Marcus Garvey's philosophy of Black racial excellence and pride has inspired Jamaica since he first began speaking, despite the fact that the liberating words are not taught as fully as they should be at an early age to give Jamaicans greater pride as Black people. Africans all over the Diaspora respect Garvey and his work and it was important and appropriate that he was declared our first National Hero.

Norman Manley and Alexander Bustamante both fought to give Jamaica political independence. Separately, yet united on different sides of the same coin, they overcame the strength of British colonialism and gave democratic political rights to the descendants of slaves. The freedom they won at Independence was not as complete as we now demand it must become with Republican status, a freedom that will remove the British royal family from claiming to be the most important influence and authority over the remnants of slavery that exist after 60 years of Independence. But they fought the battle and won it for Jamaica. (And by the way, there is a major campaign for Manley to be joined by his son Michael in the pantheon of Heroes, that would make them the first such family in the world, I am sure.)

Our National Heroine Queen Nanny represents the freedom fighters who challenged and fought British slavery. The fact that she did not sign the Peace Treaty because she felt her fellow Maroons should have continued fighting until slavery was abolished, endears her to us and moves her a step away from the tainted reputation Maroons have earned for obeying the Treaty clause that gave freedom only to those who had fought and won it, demanding the return of any slaves who tried to join them after the Treary was signed.

So we have our present Heroes, to which the callers ask for Miss Lou, Usain Bolt, Jimmy Cliff and Bob Marley to be added. I don't see that any of them have fought and won battles for Jamaica.

Louise Bennett-Coverly epitomixed and memorialixed the peasant, market woman of a very recent past, speaking the native patois born from a time when standard English was not fully comprehended by slaves imported from many different African languages. Miss Lou removed the shame of patois with her amusing and entertaining usage, and in time even made us proud to claim it as our native language.

But until lectures at the University's faculties of Law, Medicine and Science are delivered in patois, Mrs. Bennett-Coverly has not fought and won a battle. She has earned a statue which is an appropriate reward and her memory will never be erased, thanks to her poetry.

Usain Bolt has earned his statue also, with a second one to come, and several abroad, not just by winning races in 3 Olympics, but by doing so with a winning personality that made Jamaica proud. Other athletes have earned their statues also for similar achievements, and there are more to come.

But, other than the national pride whose memory becomes a more and more distant history as other athletic superstars male and female - fill Half Way Tree with cheering crowds and pride, what has Usain brought Jamaica's development? He is a proud memory, but while he is alive there is still more he can do for Jamaica that will make children remember him in decades to come as more than just one of Jamaica's many fast runners, a category that includes Arthur Wint, Merlene Ottey and Shelly-Ann Fraser-Price.

Usain is young. There is still time for him to do more, good and bad. Wait until he is gone to assess his contribution to the development of Jamaica.

Is Jimmy Cliff's singing better than any of the many hundreds of singers Jamaica has given the world since Millie Small hit the global Top Ten? Is his value as a National Hero better because he starred in a movie? If it's Jimmy's role in *"The Harder They Come"* that qualifies him, we must remember that Jimmy acted a role written by Trevor Rhone and Perry Henzell, and Henzell deserves as much honour as Jimmy for making a brilliant film that opened Jamaican Rasta-Reggae-ganja culture to the world.

Jimmy is not yet dead, so there is still time for him to announce a national fund financed by the million$$ he has earned by both his voice and the fame the film gave him. If singing quality is a qualification, then what about Toots Hibbert, Dennis Brown and all the others?

What about Peter Tosh, who may be highly praised in decades to come when his Legalize His activism is acknowledged for inspiring a ganja industry that achieves its goal of superceding the national income of today's tourism. And let us not forget Bunny Wailer, who wrote some of the songs as one of the three Wailers that came to national and international attention. Yes, Barbados produced one music superstar, so they have a right to honour Rihanna. Jamaica has produced hundreds. We can't choose just one.

However, the call for honouring Marley recognizes, as it rightly should, the very important role RASTAFARI has played in the development of Jamaica. From being a scorned, despised and downtrodden group of believers, Rastafari has shown itself to be a vibrant cultural and spiritual belief that has produced a music that has overtaken the world.

It is an indisputable fact that the existence of RASTAFARI culture has enlivened Jamaica's tourism industry and the music produced by its practitioners has given Jamaica a special affection and respect globally. UNESCO has declared Reggae a world cultural treasure, and there are hundreds of reggae concerts and shows in countries around the world.

"The Harder They Come" gave the world a look at the uniqueness of Jamaican culture and its Rasta-reggae-ganja culture that made Jamaica famous. Like it or not, the image of Jamaica created by that film, has remained. Bob Marley was not in the film, nor was his music. In fact, Marley's fame came from the co-creator of the film, Chris Blackwell, who put the Island Records publicity machine and money behind the Wailers and Bob, after Jimmy Cliff turned down his offer of a new contract when the film became a hit.

I love Bob Marley, but how will we explain the moral aspects of Bob's life to our children as a National Hero? We all know about Bob having several children outside his marriage (two women gave birth to two of his children within months of each other) and the scandal remains of his affair with another baby-mother who defied the nation's boycott of apartheid South Africa to win a beauty contest.

These are not good examples. Then again, how will we explain to our children why Bob Marley's family, has not used any of the money that keeps him top of the list of the wealthiest dead celebrities to establish a school, a hospital, an old people"s home with their wealth, that will increase even more with such an development? Bob has earned a lot from his fame and his wealth and Jamaicans can be glad to say he is one of us, like Miss Lou, Usain and Jimmy. But National Hero?

Instead, I say let Bob, and all the Rasta and reggae heroes be recognized in one National Hero Award for RASTAFARI. Rastafari has been the central spine of Jamaican culture and it deserves to be recognized for what it has given Jamaica as the world's newest religion, a culture, a national reputation and even income. The heroes of Rastafari outshine even Marley.

How can we put Marley over Leonard 'The first Rasta' Howell, who established the first example of Rastafari communal life at Pinnacle, or Ras Boanagers - Bongo Watto who took Rastafari teachings to the Caribbean islands and to Africa,, or Prince Emannuel of the Boboshanti, whose endless letters to the Queen of England, her Prime Ministers, the United Nations and Jamaica's Governors General asking for reparations and repatriation are legendary.

We can call the name of Count Ossie, who put the Mystic Revelation of Rastafari drums on to popular music and created the first authentic Rasta Reggae hit song, and Ras Sam Brown who was bold enough to stand in a General Election and show that Rastafari citizens had a right to claim political rights. What about the Rastas who inspired University professors to call for a Mission to Africa and who traveled there to examine the possibility of repatriation? Bob Marley was a youth with short hair, when all that was happening that inspired him to become a Rasta.

Though Jamaica ignores the fact, the world posts Red, Gold and Green flags and colours whenever Jamaica is mentioned. The costume of a current beauty queen recently raised irate comments because its main colours were Red, Gold and Green. Several contestantants in the annual ritual have worn dreadlocks. Jamaica has become identified as a Rasta country. We can acknowledge it.

So I say that, in my opinion, Jamaica should take a step as unique as Barbados did in declaring its own unusual National Hero, and declare RASTAFARI its next National Hero.

WHAT DOES AFRICA MEAN TO RASTAFARI?
<u>December 6, 2011</u>

Ethiopia, Darfur, Congo, Somalia, Sudan, Zimbabwe, Ghana, Kenya, Nigeria ... what does Africa mean to I&I Rastafari?

Is Africa just an emotional magnet, a name we call whenever we wish to claim our history, origin and identity as Black-skinned people? Or are I&I Rastafari eyes wide open to see Africa as the reality the continent is — a collection of nations plagued with more negative connotations than positive stories?

I open for discussion the opinion that in claiming our right of return to the Motherland, Rastafari have not truly identified Africa as a continent that needs our political intervention, care and attention more urgently than we need a place to establish a house and garden. For many years Rastafari have being sitting by "The Rivers of Babylon" chanting Repatriation. Is this only lip service or an emotional outburst?

Over the years Rastafari have discussed Africa more as a place to satisfy our needs for a home among people of the same race and heritage, than as a place to which we owe a responsibility to get involved in solving the national issues that keep the Continent poor and underdeveloped. We read of China and India investing in Africa to satisfy their countries need for raw materials, food and industrial wealth, never as a place for their citizens to reside. If China has invested so much wealth in Africa, how is it that they have never sought to establish the kind of communities in Africa that Rastafari in the West seek to create?

It is worth looking here at how China's presence in beautiful, politically stable Jamaica through its massive economic investments in the sugar and bauxite industries, and as builders of a multi-billion-dollar road system, was preceded less than 5 decades ago by the quiet but equally massive immigration of new Chinese residents as grocery and wholesale shop owners who systematically applied for Jamaican citizenship to ensure their right of abode, even before they learnt to speak English or Patois.

It is worth looking also at the fact that these grocery and wholesale shops have led to the eradication of the indigenous sidewalk stalls from which poor Jamaicans used to earn a daily living by selling loose cigarettes, bun-and-cheese and children's lunch snacks that are now replaced by Chinese wholesale shops selling the same goods just as cheaply.

Is it because China and India see clearly that living in Africa means living with all of Africa's problems: endemic malaria and other mortal diseases, lack of agricultural and sanitary water, lack of roads and communications infrastructure, lack of educational opportunities and, most glaring of all, an almost continent-wide lack of moral, incorrupt and visionary leadership.

Rastafari, as a Nation in Exile, has not collectively made an input into the work being done to eradicate malaria – the continent's most prevalent disease — as UNICEF, the Bill & Melinda Gates Foundation, and movie stars Angelina Jolie and Brad Pitt have done. Rastafari, whether collectively or individually, has not taken a political stand with the residents of the Nigerian oil delta, whose lives and livelihood have been destroyed by Shell's numerous oil spills that are ten times larger than the Gulf of Mexico oil spill that captured the world's attention via live underwater cameras for so many months in 2010.

Rastafari has not collectively spoken out to the leaders of the inhuman genocidal war in Sudan. Rastafari has not pointed out the reasons why former Somali fishermen have taken to hijacking the ships that pass through the seas around their country, where the fish population has been decimated by trawlers from rich nations such as Japan. Rastafari has not intervened in the Congo, where children are enslaved to dig for precious metals to make expensive smart phones, computers and aircraft. It takes the Catholic Pope to shift attention from his church's homosexual scandals and condemn the voodoo sacrifices of children in Benin. Rastafari has not commented on Ethiopia's war with Eritrea, nor its Government's leasing of vast acres of agricultural land to India to grow food for export only to India.

Year after year leading Rastafari such as Mutabaruka keep insisting that we should emigrate to Africa. Yet, year after year, none of these leading Rastafari do what they insist we must do – move to Africa. If they did, they could show example and guidance for others less prosperous than they. Instead, only Rita Marley moved to Africa, and she soon returned to live comfotably in the USA.

Rastafari is insisting that all Black people in the West should find the way to emigrate to Africa and establish private homesteads, such as has been established on Selassie's gift of land in Sheshemane, Ethiopia. There, Ethiopia's Omoro government, unable to comprehend Rastafari worship of a leader they have discredited, has turned much of the land bequeathed by H.I.M. over to their native population. That has led to an ongoing digital dialogue about Rastafari future in Ethiopia that has no resolution and cannot have, unless and until Rastafari religious, economic and political beliefs are understood and accepted by the world.

While other issues become international news, Rastafari has not yet learned how to bring their issues to the international news media. Efforts to have a voice in the African Union are reduced to efforts to enthrone one or other Rastafari individuals as as spokespersons in one or other of the AU's forums. Efforts to arrive at a consensus Rastafari opinion on any topic of importance, are thwarted by email discussions that inevitably stall on the question of how much interaction Rastafari should have with the 'white' world of former colonial masters. Little attention is paid to the reality that the world is now a global village in which people of all races have been drawn to Rastafari through their harmony with the Rastafari slogan of Peace and Love, and who can and should therefore be used as messengers to their racial and national communities to help achieve Rastafari goals.

I once had the privilege of asking Fidel Castro the question: "You once said that you looked forward to a time when all Cubans would work not for money, but for the good of each other as humans. Has Cuba achieved this yet?" The great leader, whose soldiers fought and died to help liberate several African nations from European colonialism, replied: "As we worked towards that goal, we realized that we had to pause and help the rest of the world achieve that goal with us first. We are still working on that."

Rastafari needs a leader with this viewpoint. It is time for Rastafari to realize that chants alone cannot resolve InI problems. We must be cognizant of the fact that the Government is on InI shoulders. It is time for Rastafari to pause and help the rest of Africa achieve its goals

THE CORAL GARDENS INCIDENT — ALSO CALLED 'A MASSACRE'

The **Coral Gardens Incident**, also known as the **Coral Gardens Atrocitiy**, the **Coral Gardens Massacre**, the **Coral Gardens riot**, and **Bad Friday** refers to a series of events that occurred in Jamaica from April 11-13 1963.

As a journalist, as a student of Jamaican history, and eventually becoming an employee of the Jamaican Ministry of Culture given the job of delivering Government's reparations for Coral Gardens to the victims and survivors, I have been able to take an in-depth view of that infamous incident in contemporary Jamaican history. I share my report here.

Following the events of April 11-13, two narratives of the Coral Gardens Incident emerged. One view held that the events of the Good Friday weekend constituted an unlawful uprising by the Rastafarians; this view was supported by contemporary media reports of the events and the statements of government officials at the time.

On the other hand, the Rastafarian community in Jamaica felt then, and still feels, that the actions of Rudolph Franklyn and his compatriots were a justified reaction to decades of persecution by the Jamaican Government through its Police, Army and a statement by then-Prime Minister Alexander Bustamante, and perceive the mass arrests that followed the Incident as an abuse of state powers, a view that has been reflected by more recent academic scholarship

Coral Gardens was part of a larger property, the Rose Hall estate which includes the famous Rose Hall mansion. This property was the site of both small-scale farming by Rastafarians, as well as the ambitions of landlords and government officials who hoped to convert the area into a tourist destination. The government and landlords saw the Rastafarians as an obstacle to their goal of re-purposing the property for tourism, and frequently sent police to evict the Rastafarians.

In one such incident in 1961, police attacked Rudolph Franklyn, shooting him six times in the stomach and leaving him for dead. Franklyn received plastic surgery in a hospital to repair his stomach, but was reportedly told by a doctor that once the plastic "rotted", his wounds would reopen and he would die. Following his surgery, Franklyn was immediately arrested on the grounds of cannabis possession and sentenced to six months in prison. After his release from prison, Franklyn reportedly swore to take revenge against the overseer who had attempted to evict him.

Raging at the multiple experiences of injustice, on his release, Rudolf Franklin conspired with two friends to take revenge by burning down the Ken Douglas Shell Station in Coral Gardens and to eliminate Edward Fowler, the eviction agent. The burning of the gas station represented the Rastafari 'burning of the Babylon system, symbolised by the State. At the time of the incident, the Government was led by newly minted Prime Minister Sir Alexander Bustamante, who became infamous for urging the police to "bring them [Rastafari] in, dead or alive." The police went on a rampage.

Following the violent altercation at the gas station, a police manhunt tracked down and killed the other Rastafarians that had been present at the skirmish. Jamaican police and military forces detained Rastafarians throughout St. James, killing and torturing many. Exact numbers are not available, but estimates place the number of detained individuals "as high as 150". Jamaican newspapers such as *The Daily Gleaner* published many articles demonizing the Rastafarians and demanding armed intervention by the state

The Coral Gardens 'uprising', described in the book *"Rudolf Franklin's Revenge"* written by Rastafari author Ras Flako, was blown out of proportion by the security forces that were becoming more and more agitated by the fact and implications of the physical self-representation of Rastafari as well as by their uncompromising cultural profile. However, upon reflection, the entire incident should have just been a storm in a teacup.

Media also originally described the events at Coral Gardens as an "uprising", and were later forced to retract their characterization of the event by the Jamaica Labour Party-led government. While only a few Rastafari were directly involved in this incident, the entire community began to be subjected to severe forms of persecution by the security forces as well as by other civil society institutions in the political backlash.

In December 2015, after decades of agitation, the local Rastafarian community finally got an official acknowledgment, through an investigation conducted by the Office of the Public Defender, that its adherents were unjustly treated in the 1963 Coral Gardens incident in Montego Bay, St James.

Public Defender Arlene Harrison Henry said the Rastafarians were subjected to "discrimination, denigration and scorn", and called for an apology and compensation to those who suffered unjustly.

" ... What our investigations found is that many Rastafarians - some of whom were not taken into custody - certainly had to trim their dreadlocks and their beards so as to avoid being taken into custody and to avoid prosecution," said Harrison Henry.

Her report was the basis on which future reparations to Rastafari for the Coral Gardens Incident were paid.

APOLOGY AND REPARATIONS BY THE JAMAICAN GOVERNMENT

In the retaliation which followed days after the Coral Gardens Incident, the Police with the help of civilians rounded up scores of men affiliated to the Rastafari movement, leaving many with severe wounds and an unknown number missing, presumed dead. The incident was the most violent of all the attacks conducted over several decades by the Jamaican state to suppress the Rastafari movement and its Afrocentric philosophy. Of them all, the Coral Gardens Incident has become an infamous and ugly landmark in Jamaican history.

Several Governments have passed in the half century since then, and despite the continuing demands by the Rastafari community and defenders of human rights, JLP and PNP Prime Ministers Bustamante, Sangster, Shearer, Manley Seaga, Patterson, Simpson-Miller and Golding have never addressed the frequent calls for an apology and compensation for the wrongs and injustices of Coral Gardens.

Finally, in 2017 the JLP government led by Prime Minister Andrew Holness, born years after the Coral Gardens Incident, decided to heed the never-ending calls for justice and reparations to be given to those who suffered in that infamous moment of Jamaican history. First the Prime Minister called together a Cabinet Sub-Committee headed by Deputy Prime Minister Horace Chang and MP Audley Shaw to receive reports and discuss what could and should be done. The Committee recommended that the Government should first issue an apology to the Rastafari Community, then offer financial compensation to the survivors of the brutality that followed the fiery event.

The Government sought a fair mechanism to determine how and to whom compensation should be paid. In 2015, Government asked the Office of the Public Defender to dig deep to locate survivors and get information on their current socio-economic and living conditions. The Office of the Public Defender underwent a careful, detailed and lengthy search and compilation of data in consultation with the Rastafari Coral Gardens Benevolent Society and the Member of Parliament for that area, and finally submitted a report to the Prime Minister in April, 2019.

On the basis of that report, it was decided that a Trust Fund of no less than $10M be established by the Administrator General to be shared among all survivors of the Coral Gardens Incident. The job of leading the work that had to be done to establish that Fund and to work with the Rastafari community to reach consensus on the matter, was placed in the hands of Minister of Culture, Gender, Entertainment & Sport Olivia Grange.

On March 21, 2017, speaking in Parliament at Gordon House, Prime Minister Holness made a historic announcement: "I committed to making an apology for what has come to be commonly referred to as the Coral Gardens incident; one which occurred at a time in our history when our society was more reflective of the colonial era. Today, I am honouring the commitment to tender an apology."

Explaining the background to the Incident, Prime Minister Holness continued: "Violence flared up at Coral Gardens leading to the death of civilians and police, significant personal injuries and destruction of property. The Rastafarian community has harboured feelings of bitterness and resentment over the years. The Coral Gardens Incident was a grave injustice. The Government acknowledges that the machinery of the Jamaican state evolved out of an era when it was considered appropriate to utilize the heavy hand of the state against citizens."

"Today, without equivocation, we apologise for what occurred in Coral Gardens. We express regret and sorrow for this chapter in our national life that was characterised by brutality, injustice and repression. It was wrong and should never be repeated," the Prime Minister stressed. "I am happy to have finally reached the point where we can discuss concrete and tangible actions, which ease some of the heavy burdens that survivors and the community had faced."

Seven months later, a document confirming the setting up of the Rastafari Coral Gardens Trust Fund by the Administrator General's Office was signed on December 19, 2019 between the Rastafari Coral Gardens Benevolent Society and the Ministry of Culture through whom the fund is forwarded from the Ministry of Finance.

At the signing, the Ministry of Culture, Gender, Entertainment and Sport transferred Twelve Million, Seven Hundred and Eighteen Thousand Dollars to the Administrator General as the first step for the setting up the Trust Fund, exceeding the $10 Million the Public Defender had proposed. So far $112 million has been deposited into the trust fund and disbursements are done on a monthly basis to the individual survivors.

Addressing the signing ceremony Minister Grange said: "I come humbly, as representative of this Administration, to take steps to right a wrong. We acknowledge that for 56 years, you — our Rastafari brothers and sisters — have lived with the physical, psychological and emotional scars of that incident at Coral Gardens and the atrocities you experienced over the years. We also know that you feel that successive governments have let you down by not sufficiently acknowledging what you have been through. We are taking steps to change that."

She informed that the Ministry had also appointed a Cultural Liaison with responsibility for Rastafari Affairs, Mrs. Barbara Blake Hannah, a known expert in Rastafari heritage, to handle matters relating to the welfare of the community. After the signing, the Cultural Liaison conducted a tour of the Granville community where many survivors of Coral Gardens lived. Her distress on seeing the poor conditions in which several lived, led the Ministry to allocate funds from its own budget to establish an Elder Care facility. for the benefit of all those survivors who did not have caregivers.

A Rastafari Coral Gardens Elder Care Home was opened at a rented property in Norwood, St. James with help from Food for The Poor, who supplied wheelchairs, the Ministry of Social Service, and furniture from private donors. All expenses and operational costs including food and medical care, are covered by the Ministry of Culture. The government has identified land that will ultimately be used to house a permanent Elder Care Home for the victims.

The Elder Care Home Opening Day was held on April 1, 2021, with a program of speeches, drumming and Rastafari chanting. The event was chaired by Dr. Horace Chang, Member of Parliament for the Constituency who is also Minister of National Security. Dr. Chang spoke out against discrimination while placing his personal respect and that of the Government towards the contributions of Rastafari citizens.

Sister Pamela Rowe—Williams, Secretary and spokesperson of the Rastafari Coral Gardens Benevolent Society, thanked the Government in a letter to Minister Grange, stating: *"On behalf of the survivors of the 1963 Coral Gardens atrocities, Rastafari Coral Gardens Benevolent Society wishes to express sincere gratitude for the fact that $78 million was recently transferred to the Rastafari Coral Gardens Trust Fund. The survivors have since received a second disbursement from the fund for which they are extremely appreciative.*

"The Benevolent Society is also thankful for the finalization of the MOU regarding support for the eldercare facility. We also received $1million through the NCR which was granted in response to our plan to implement a day-care program for other survivors who will not be housed at the facility. It will be used for that purpose when the facility is in operation.

"We also wish to express our appreciation for the grant of five hundred thousand dollars ($500,000.00) which we received through the National Council on Reparations for sponsorship of our commemoration event. RCGBS looks forward to continuing a close working relationship with your Ministry."

The relationship between the Government and the Coral Gardens community continues to be strong. Speaking at a recent meeting of the St. James Municipal Corporation where members of the Rastafari community witnessed the grandson of the late Emperor of Ethiopia, Haile Selassie, Prince Ermias Sahle Selassie, being presented with the Key to the City of Montego Bay, Gregory Taylor, Chairman of the Rastafari Coral Gardens Benevolent Society said that some commitments made in subsequent discussions with the government have not yet materialized, but he nevertheless expressed his gratitude for the commitments that have already been honoured.

Responding, Minister Grange said: While there are still some outstanding matters to be dealt with, including transfer of promised land, this matter is proceeding through the system and a final handover of a Title for land to construct a permanent facility, as well as land for agricultural development will soon take place. She says she is proud to be a member of the Government that has done its best to correct the injustices meted out to the Rastafarian community at the 1963 Coral Gardens incident."

Minister Grange also informed that in keeping with the principle of cultural preservation and in addition to the commitments made to the Rastafari community for the Coral Gardens Incident, six lots at the property at Pinnacle in St Catherine have been purchased by the Government and declared by the Jamaica National Heritage Trust as a protected heritage site to be developed as a Rastafari Heritage and Cultural Centre.

As Prime Minister Holness said in his 2017 statement to Parliament: "While we know this apology cannot erase the brutality, oppression and injustice, I am comforted by the willingness of the Rastafari Coral Gardens Benevolent Society to keep the dialogue going," he said. "I wish to thank the members of the Rastafari Coral Gardens Benevolent Society for your unswerving commitment to this cause, your patience and "overstanding", as we move forward together in faith."

TWO VERSIONS OF THE CORAL GARDENS STORY
1. HORACE CAMPBELL
A powerful testimony by Jamaican academic and writer Horace Campbell was published April 12, 2013 to commemorate the 50th anniversary of the Coral Gardens uprising combining personal

recollections and memories of that fateful Easter weekend, with a penetrating analysis of the deep-seated causes of the conflict. Excerpts of Campbell's article (full text is available online) are published here:

It was fifty years ago on April 11, 1963 when the Jamaican state used an altercation at Coral Gardens on the outskirts of Montego Bay, Jamaica, to mount a violent campaign against the Rastafarian community in Western Jamaica. The events of April 12,1963 involved a group of Rastafarians and at the end of the incident, eight were killed and two policemen perished in the incident. The brethren had claimed freedom of movement for themselves and for other oppressed Jamaicans. They were being prevented from walking along the areas of the Coast close to the Half Moon Bay Hotel. These areas were being segregated in order to make the Montego Bay area ready for international investments in tourism.

Montego Bay and St. James at the period of independence in 1962 and examine the social relationships between the brethren and the dominant social elements who called on the police to keep the thoroughfare of Coral Gardens and Rose Hall free from the presence of bearded men walking through to Flower Hill and Salt Springs.

The peoples of Jamaica acceded to Independence on August 6, 1962. The people of St, James in the Western part of Jamaica, as in all parts of the island society at that moment, were searching for levers to break the power of the plantation owners. In 1962 the largest landowner was the Custos of St James, Sir Francis Moncrieff Kerr-Jarrett who owned numerous sugar plantations. Kerr-Jarrett (1886-1968), had been among the most active of the planter class in Jamaica opposing Marcus Garvey in the twenties and thirties. Together with H.G. DeLisser, from another planter family, these colonial operators had opposed Garveyism and the nationalist ideas of Jamaica.

In the years prior to independence, Francis Kerr-Jarrett had made numerous appeals to the Governor of Jamaica, Sir Hugh Foot and later Kenneth Blackburne, to crack down on the growing Rastafari movement. He continuously petitioned the Governor and the colonial office to clamp down on the Rastafari who he described as 'an undesirable sect' and urged the Governor to do everything in his power to discourage their activities. Through the activism of Kerr-Jarrett, the colonial Special Branch police had placed numerous Rastafari camps under surveillance and had used the Vagrancy laws from the period of enslavement against the camps of the Rastafari.

Barnett Estates was owned by the Kerr-Jarrett family and dominated the economy of St James prior to the boom in tourism. The estates on the other side of the town were being overtaken by the desire to turn the Rose Hall and Iron shore estates into a tourist resort. In 1954, a group of leading international capitalists had come together to claim a 400-acres hundred portion of land to establish the Half Moon Bay Hotel in the bay which was previously been the port for the offloading of sugar for the Rose Hall estates.

The Rose Hall Plantation had been the scene of brutality for hundreds of years and H.G DeLisser had written a novel celebrating one of the owners of that plantation, Annie Palmer. H.G DeLisser had been an activist in the Jamaica Imperial Society and had served as the editor of *The Daily Gleaner* newspaper of Jamaica. His family owned large parcels of land in the parishes of St James, Trelawney and Hanover. The continuities from the period of slavery was most manifest in the fact that Harold DeLisser had been named the first managing director of this plantation turned hotel, which was to grow with a 18-hole golf course across the road from the hotel and included redevelopment of the area around Coral Gardens to become a major tourist resort.

Opposition to the planter class by the poor and oppressed had taken many forms and it was from this part of Jamaica that nationalism had taken a consistent and clear form of independent working people's organization

Rudolph Franklyn was continuously harassed by the police in a climate of hostility that had been contrived by Kerr-Jarrett, Walter Fletcher, the Delissers and the colonial forces. For the owners of the new and expanding properties, the presence of the Rastas had been a disincentive for investors. Numerous calls were being made for barriers to the movement of the Rastafari in the Coral Gardens area. The ambitious 'developers' aspired to prevent 'undesirables' from walking through private property.

By 1962 Franklyn had mobilized other small farmers who had been moved to become part of the Rastafari movement. One way of coercing the Rastafari was through the Dangerous Drugs law and Franklyn had been arrested for possession of ganja. It is now known that Franklyn was seeking to do small farming in the area around Flower Hill and Salt Spring. For the tourist developers, the sight of Franklyn and other brethren walking along the road across from Half-Moon was offensive.

Independence was supposed to give all Jamaicans freedom of speech, freedom of worship, freedom of movement and the right to a decent life. All of these freedoms had been denied to the Rastafari with constant harassment. After the 1960 uprisings with the Henry brothers this harassment had increased. The British military had been brought to Jamaica to put down the rebellion of small group that had launched armed struggles for independence. Coming one year after the Cuban revolution, the British colonialists were nervous about the possible spark of revolution in the English-speaking Caribbean.

One police officer has written for the Jamaican elite his version of the confrontation and this book now serves to distort the climate of hostility that had been bred by the white planter class against the Jamaican small farmers who had turned to the ideas and philosophy of peace and love. These Rastafari had been provoked, harassed and they sought to defend themselves and for this they were shot down.

2. SELBOURNE REID, POLICE OFFICER

The Coral Gardens Incident *seen through the eyes of one of the Policemen who were first respondents to the carnage, and later to the reactions of the citizens of Montego Bay after hearing reports of what had taken place. His book is sold online.*

……The gas station attendant said he hastily opened a door to the back of the station, ran into a nearby cane field behind the gas station and his himself. While we were talking to this man, my party and I received a report which caused some of us to go to the adjacent Edgewater Inn Hotel.

Salesperson Chopped to Death

There on the motel premises I saw the body of a man of Caucasian decent, lying on the floor. This body was later identified as that of Kenneth Marsh, a sales clerk from Kingston. I still remember looking down at the body dressed in a white shirt and black necktie lying on the ground with what appeared to be large lacerated wounds all over. This scene is indelibly written in my mind as if it were yesterday. Marsh we later learned was apparently going towards his car when he met the group of Rastafarians, wo attacked and chopped him to death, then left his lifeless body lying on the floor of the model in a pool of blood. The body was reminiscent of a rat which was killed by a farmer, who used his machete to shop it and left it lying on the ground to drown in its own blood.

We were informed that a security guard at the motel was also attached and seriously wounded. He escaped by running away and hiding himself behind a tree. Information received is that as he was being pursued or chased by the group of Rastamen, he shouted and alerted the management and staff as well as the guests at the motel and they telephoned the police.

Additional information disclosed that some members of this group of Rasta men were armed with machetes, spears, bow and arrows, axes and a few cat-o-nine (that is a whip made out of cow hide and small strands of wire plaited together). There were also little pieces of metal stitched unto the many thongs of this whip. This was the type of whip used in the days of slavery to beat the slaves. Other members of this group were armed with bolas (a type of primitive weapon originated in Africa) and other primitive weapons.

Before we began our search for this gang of murderous men, we received information that this group of Rastafarian attacked Mr. Edward Fowler who was the overseer of the Kerr Jarrett's properties in Rose Hall and Coral Gardens. Fowler was on his way to tether his goats... as he was accustomed to do, when he was attacked. He was chopped and killed and his body left in the pathway. Mr Stewart, another overseer on the Tryall estate, was also seriously injured when the gang attacked his home. He escaped death after he shot and injured one of his assailants. We were informed that this overseer's home was being attached when he fired is pistol at the attackers. He escaped with his family through a rear door to hide himself in a nearby sugar cane field. From information received, the group of Rastafarian men chopped out the door of Mr. Stewart's house, went inside and searched for him. When they did not see him they set his house on fire.

Hell Broke Loose and Chaos Reigned

At about 7.30 a.m. that morning I was sitting in the back of the lead land rover with five other Constables. Inspector Fisher was sitting in the front passenger seat of the land rover being driven by a Corporal of police. Just as the vehicle was negotiating a bend, I saw some Rastafarian men coming towards the vehicle from the right hand or south eastern side of the vehicle as well as in front of the vehicle. They were running towards the vehicle and simultaneously shooting arrows from the bows they carried. They were also armed with other missiles. Some of them were throwing at us spears, made of long lengths of iron with sharpened points. One member of this group had a cowhide – whip or cat-o-mine, which when he flashed it in the air it made sounds like the explosion of small arms. The corporal who was standing behind me was about to fall, having been chopped by a Rasta-man who apparently passed behind me and between this constable and myself.

Some of my co-workers thought that the man who chopped this constable might have been the leader of the troupe Randolph Franklyn. Franklyn knew this constable, as he was his (Franklyn's) guard when he Franklyn was in police custody and a patient in the Montego Bay hospital a few months before. This constable regularly did guard duty as the Montego Bay hospital and was assigned to guard Franklyn. Franklyn apparently did not intend to kill this constable.

Anyway, this constable was chopped across his shoulder close to the back of his neck. He was bleeding all over on the back of his shirt. I thought of offering some assistance to him but realizing the danger to myself, I quickly abandoned the idea as being futile and foolhardy. I ran away carrying my empty rifle. I ran with my rifle that in case it should become necessary, the empty rifle according to my training could be a saviour in 'hand to hand fighting' should such eventuality become a reality.

Detective Corporal Melbourne

As I started to run from the scene, I saw Detective Melbourne – the idol of the citizens of Montego Bay – get out of his Police patrol car and was advancing to the front where the vehicle in which I had travelled stopped and where Fisher was on the ground. Melbourne had his service revolver drawn. As he ran towards Fisher, a spear struck him in his head and he fell. Immediately Melbourne fell, I saw a Rastafarian like a hungry scavenger with legions of demons from Hell swooped down upon him and began to chop him in the head and upper torso.

The animated spirit of life in me immediately became non-existent as I witnessed the life of a decent, peaceful, respectable, helpful and loving men, being chopped out of his body. As I ran down the tract and away from the slaughter, I felt angry, disgusted, frustrated and disoriented. I felt this way as I reflected on the horror and stupidity on the part of John Fisher. How his action would affect hundred and may be thousands of people then and in the future.

Detective Corporal Melbourne was one of the two Detective photographers in Montego Bay at the time. He was a very hard working police officer. He was loved and admired by everyone who knew him including some criminals. Criminals respected him as he always treated law offenders fairly and with respect. Melbourne, like myself and many other police officers of the 1960s believed that when a man commit an infraction against the law, Policemen should not take the committal of such offence personally. The policeman should execute his duty fairly, politely, efficiently and effectively.

Melbourne was an honest fair-minded and helpful man. He was a man who would always find time to help, teach and answer most questions other policemen may have, particularly the younger men like myself. After I saw the manner he was being chopped, there was no doubt in my mind that he was killed. He died leaving his wife and family, relatives and a host of friends. His body when retrieved was mutilated beyond recognition. We could not even take photographs of the body as any photographs taken could have caused much trauma to those who see the photographs of his mangled body.

Constable E.W. Campbell

Constable E.W. Campbell, my squad-mate from training school was another of those who was seriously injured that morning. He came out of the land rover ahead of me. He ran from the land rover and tried to go between the strands of a barbed wire fence in the act of escaping. He put part of his body between the strands of wires and was in the act of pulling the other portion o f his body including his head between the wires when his shirt was caught between the strands. As he tried to clear himself from the wire, he was chopped in the head with a machete by a Rasta-man. The wound caused his brains to protrude. He survived but will remain a vegetable for the rest of his life. He was engaged at the time to be married to his school day's sweetheart, a marriage that obviously did not materialize. Campbell is alive but even forty years after his injuries, he was still being obliged to be making petition to the Jamaican government for FINANCIAL ASSISTANCE to help defray his living expenses.

I am convinced to this day that my escape unscratched that morning was by means of Divine Intervention and from the prayers of my mother as well as other people who loved me. I had become a Christian a few months before and was a member of the Assemblies of God church on Barnett Street in Montego Bay.

Reinforcement Despatched

At about 8:45 a.m. the same day 'Black Thursday' from the police station at Barnett Street, another party of police officers was dispatched to the scene in the Coral Gardens hills. Obviously it was of paramount importance that the police return to the scene of the crime.

As the land rover ascended the hillsides, driving along the winding path, several civilians on foot and some traveling in their own vehicles joined the trail behind us. The road on the hillside was a narrow track with no space where a vehicle could turn around or reverse. Thus we travelled in a single file at a crawling pace along the hillside. As we drove along, it was moving to see the long trail of civilian volunteers who joined the police party. The citizens were apparently impacted by the fact that tragedy had come to their beautiful town of Montego Bay and disrupted their economic lifeline 'tourism'. They were determined to preserve this economic lifeline and catching these men was a worthwhile and popular desire The apparent thought was "If these men were not caught everyone would life in fear. Therefore 'these Rasta criminals must be caught at all costs'.

Most of the police officers that were in the parties that morning ran away from the scene. Some men ran to the main road, which was about three miles away from the scene of the slaughter. At the main road they obtained public transportation back to the station. It was subsequently discovered that two police officers that originated from St. Mary, a Parish in the North eastern section of Jamaica and approximately one hundred miles away from Montego Bay, ran away from the scene and was declared missing. One of them was located at his home in Saint Mary many days after and he was still in hiding. It was rumoured that he ran from the scene of slaughter in Coral Gardens hills to the main road. As he reached the main road, he saw a public passenger bus going to his hometown in St. Mary. He got onto the bus and went to his home. He was still dazed and frightened when he was located about three weeks later. …. He was fearful that a Rasta-man would find him and try to hurt him.

The other constable ran away from the scene of the tragedy in the Coral Gardens hills for about five miles to the Montego bay hospital. On reaching the hospital and seeing the medical personnel he fainted. Still in a state of stupor, he was asked to say what was his complaint. Wiping away tears from his eyes, he said, "The Rasta-man chopped at me and missed". He apparently thought it impossible for him not to have been injured. He just ran all the way to the hospital and fainted as he reached and saw the medical people.

Psychological Effects

The incident had a great psychological effect on us. Many of us police officers had nightmares for many weeks and months later. I would oftentimes wake up in the middle of nights frightened and nervous. I was so affected that I was afraid to sleep. For a period of about three weeks after the incident, I could not sleep. During this time I lost over ten pounds in weight. I do not recommend to anyone this weight loss program but it worked for me at that time.

Citzens Vigilante Justice

The Jamaica Defence Force for the first time since Jamaica's independence in 1962 was called out to assist and work alongside the police in the maintaining of law and order in Jamaica. They were called into action to assist in law and order a few times during the previous three years to assist the police during the Henry's attempt to overthrow the Jamaican Government in the late 1950s. (Daily Gleaner April 1958). The police and military personnel tried to maintain law and order in the principal commercial areas as well as searching for the escaped cultists.

While this was being done by the Law enforcement personnel, the citizens formed vigilante groups and began to route and flush out every one of the remaining members of this terrorist group. They apparently thought the police was not vigilant enough so the formed citizen's vigilante groups. These citizens' vigilante groups apprehended anyone who wore a bears of locks their hair. Consequently, even professionals who were accustomed to wear their beard as a status symbol and did not embrace the Rastafarian beliefs and culture had to cut their locks and shaved their beards to avoid being arrested and manhandled by the citizens. *"It matters not if the bearded man black white brown or yellow. His beard would get him arrested and no one would ask why or help. His beard could be slender as a nail. By Vigilante justice he goes to hail"*

This was one of the few times in Jamaica's history when the colour of one's skin was of no significance. Light skinned bearded men were even more suspicious because of Claudius and Ronald Henry attempt to overthrow the Jamaican Government many months before. Both of the Henrys were Caucasian in complexion. People of such complexion in Jamaica were referred to as 'light skinned. The jails all over St. James and even some adjacent parishes were filled with prisoners, mostly bearded men. Some were not even Rasta men.

In the process, four Rastafarians from the gang of terrorists were captured, arrested and charged with various breaches of the law including the murder of Detective Melbourne. For many days it was chaos in Montego Bay. At the time of the incident, the Government was led by newly minted Prime Minister Sir Alexander Bustamante, who became infamous for urging the police to *"bring them [Rastafari] in, dead or alive."*

As police the land rover ascended the hillsides, driving along the winding path, several civilians on foot and some traveling in their own vehicles joined the trail behind us. The road on the hillside was a narrow track with no space where a vehicle could turn around or reverse. Thus we travelled in a single file at a crawling pace along the hillside. As we drove along, it was moving to see the long trail of civilian volunteers who joined the police party. The citizens were apparently impacted by the fact that tragedy had come to their beautiful town of Montego Bay and disrupted their economic lifeline 'tourism'. They were determined to preserve this economic lifeline and catching these men was a worthwhile and popular desire The apparent thought was "If these men were not caught everyone would life in fear. Therefore 'these Rasta criminals must be caught at all costs'.

This was the apparent invisible or latent mission statement of these citizens and they were doing their part in helping the police to catch the criminals. These wonderful civic minded citizens rose toa n occasion in which they felt obligated and motivated to be involved, as at that time the memories of the 'Red Hills Gantt' – a group of Jamaicans led by the Rev. Claudius Henry and his son Ronald Henry, who attempted a few years before to overthrow the Jamaican government, was still current in the citizens' minds. The Citizens demonstrated a love and concern for their town and country. They felt that the actions of the Rasta men were barbarous and unacceptable. They citizens were not prepared to sit back and do nothing, so they joined the Police party.

What was it that caused such citizens' reaction to the actions of this group of Rasta men? The answers to such and similar questions may lie in the annals of Jamaica's history and to this end, I would like to suggest an historical review for investigation. Be it understood, that nothing I shall say in this context should be construed or taken as a justification for the atrocious actions of this group of Rastafarians. There was no justification for their criminal actions and wonton behaviour.

There is a possibility that they may have been exposed to the ideology and doctrine of the 'Young Radicals' otherwise called the 'Young Socialist Group' which caused them to become confused. On the other hand, the actions of the citizens' vigilante groups were very disturbing. The actions of the Rastafarians were demonic, foolish and misguided. I will however attempt to link history and economics with the actions of the disenfranchised people in any society. Based on this premise, we may find some similarities among these Rasta men and other groups of oppressed peoples everywhere.

DURBAN MEMORIES
Published July 2020

I was at home one day in 2001, when the phone rang.

"Mrs. Hannah, I am calling from Canada on behalf of the United Nations. We have been trying to contact you for 3 weeks. We have money for you to buy your ticket to South Africa immediately to attend the World Conference Against Racism!"

I hardly remembered that I had applied as the Rasta Information Service to cover the World Conference, because as a Rasta I knew Reparations was going to be a major issue. I deeply wanted to add my voice to the many voices I knew would be there, but it was almost like putting a message in a bottle and casting it out to sea with hope.

I had been inspired to fight for this particular Rastafari cause by the works of Jah Lloyd, a Rastafari elder who had been the most outspoken Rasta on Reparations. Jah Lloyd had died a short while before, on his first trip to Africa, leaving a vacant space where action was badly needed. Speaking up about Reparations would be as if I was picking up his fallen banner and hoisting it high again.

I hardly thought my application would have been accepted, but it was! There was money waiting for me and a flight booked to travel to Durban via London. I just had time to get a malaria shot and pack a bag.

I arrived in Durban in the midst of delegates from all over the world, people wearing national dress of many styles and colours. Before leaving Jamaica I had informed the Ministry of Foreign Affairs of my invitation. To my great delight and honour, they invited me to be an official member of the Jamaican delegation, glad to have a Rasta in their group. Senior Foreign Affairs official Sheila Monteith (now an Ambassador) took me under her wing, explaining what to do, while Jamaican Ambassador Stafford Neil greeted me warmly.

The most senior member of the Jamaican delegation was Ambassador Dudley Thompson, one of the creators of the famous Abuja Declaration and an international pioneer of the movement for Reparations, who was very well known in Africa and Pan-African circles as the lawyer who defended Jomo Kenyatta at his Mau Mau trials. I had known him from I was a child, and he was glad to see me and proud of my Afrocentric activities.

The Jamaican delegation's seats in the Conference Assemby Hall were beside Japan, whose delegates hardly showed up each day. To the left of their empty seats was the delegation from Israel that included a brown-skinned lady, who I assumed was one of the many Ethiopians who had migrated to Israel. I wore my white Ethiopian dresses and shama headwraps every day, so on the first day the lady greeted me in Amharic, confirming my assumption that she was Ethiopian. I had to smile and tell her I was Jamaican and my Amharic was very limited, but she had heard of Rastafari, so I began a very amicable relationship with the Israeli delegation thereafter.

A problem that kept arising at the Conference was that every debate on every topic on the agenda soon brought the issue of Reparations to the surface and when this problem eventually seemed likely to derail the entire Conference, the topic of Reparations was moved into a new plenary containing the most passionate African and Caribbean supporters of Reparations, as well as the representatives of European enslaving nations who were being called to answer.

Ambassador Thompson and I were delegated to represent Jamaica in this plenary and found myself in company with delegates from the Caribbean including Ras Iral Jabari, David Commisong and Hilary Beckles of Barbados, as well as delegates from Africa. The plenary contained many angry verbal confrontations between representatives of the Black people who had been enslaved and the White people who had enslaved us, with many attempts to bargain for commitments from the White nations, which they were determined not to give.

It was a hard struggle, but by the end we finally managed to agree on what should be included in the Conference's statement on Reparations. I am proud to report that at my insistence, with support from Ambassador Thompson, we were able to have the list of Forms of Reparations include a special recognition of Reparations with Repatriation and the words: "*The Welcomed return and re-settlement in Africa of descendants of enslaved Africans*" were added as the very last item on that important and historic list.

Being in Africa was a special and wonderful experience and Durban was beautiful. It was good to see Black people moving about in control of such a developed city, just as it was shocking for me to see poor, ragged White people begging at the stop lights. Jamaica seemed so far away!

To have touched my feet on the Motherland was very special to me. It hit me the hardest one night as I sat in a speaker's tent at the People's Village outside the Conference Center, looking down at my feet on the red earth of Durban and seeing how different it was to any earth I had seen at home in Jamaica. It was African earth, I realised. I was here in Africa with my feet on the earth of my ancestors! I really had to think about that.

As I was thinking, a woman with her head covered in a flowing scarf came into the tent, saw us and came over to us with tears streaming down her face. She bowed down before us, saying over and over "Thank you for coming to South Africa my Sister! Thank you for coming to South Africa my brother! Thank you for coming to South Africa!!!" I looked at her, but she wasn't mad. She really meant it. "Thank you for coming!"

Tears rolled down my face and my heart was overwhelmed by the fact that it was many, many generations ago that people related to me had lived in Africa, had touched their feet to this African earth, but had never known me, their stolen daughter. I cried for all the family in Africa I had never met, and I cried for the family who had been taken to Jamaica who I also had never met.

I felt alone and lonely, my mother and father were dead, I had no more link with Africa. All I had now to link me with Africa was my son. I hoped I had made the African blood in his multi-racial mixture strong enough to endure and keep the link alive.

Heading into the Conference Center in the morning that the Final Report was presented, walking towards me was the Conference Chairman, UN Ambassador Mary Robinson, former Prime Minister of Ireland. To my surprise, as we passed each other she looked me in the eyes with a smile and winked.

It wasn't till I saw the Conference daily newspaper a little later that I realised she knew who I was because she had seen my photo on the paper's front page in an interview in which I had said: "I am the first member of my family to have touched foot in Africa for 300 years. I cried when I arrived. We need Reparations so we can return home."

The World Conferencee Against Racism turned out to be an unofficial sitting of the United Nations, as senior diplomats and politicians of every country were present. Of them all, the presence of Fidel Castro was the most historic, but the most newsworthy personality was Madeline Albright, the US Secretary of State who headed the American delegation that the world had expected Colin Powell to lead. The fight against racism took another road at the Conference in an incident that made big news – the walkout of the US and Israeli delegations after disagreeing with the continued hammering of a resolution that equated Zionism with racism.

In a co-incidence that needs to go on record, the walkout took place at the same time as a meeting I had arranged - with approval of Ambassador Neil - for the Israeli delegation to formally meet with the Jamaican delegation to discuss ways I believed Jamaica could help in bringing a peaceful resolution to the Palestinian situation. As we sat waiting, Ambassador Neil's phone rang cancelling the meeting without giving a reason.

    We all left the meeting room and went to the lift – only to find as the doors opened that we had to step back to give way to Madeline Albright and her US delegation walking out of the Conference!! We soon discovered the Israeli delegation were doing exactly the same thing!

    Leaving Durban, the flight stopped at Cape Town en route to London. An hour later they informed us that the flight was cancelled and would be re-scheduled for 2 days later. I was tired and sad to be away from my son for so long. I cried.

    A kind airline person booked me into a lovely hotel suite and I woke the next morning with a beautiful view across the sea to Robben Island where Nelson Mandela had been imprisoned. Then the kind lady booked me on a flight that day to Fort Lauderdale, telling me the only problem was that it took 17 hours. It was the longest flight I have ever held my breath for, but I was glad to be going home. I went to bed and fell asleep immediately.

    I was still deep in slumber next morning when I was awakened by my son shouting and calling me to the television. There before our eyes a plane flew into the Twin Towers, and exploded in flames. Minutes later another one did!!!

    It was 9/11 – the most famous day in aviation history!

In the global crisis that followed, all air travel was halted for days. I would have been stuck somewhere in the world for days, if I had not taken the 17 hour flight back home.

I have always wondered if it was mere coincidence that 9/11 happened right after the US walked out of the World Conference Against Racism!

Looking back on 20 years, it seems that so little has happened that so many good people worked so hard to achieve in Durban. Racism is still a monster devouring the hearts and lives of Black people everywhere, reaching from the poorest to the highest families. The war for Reparations for Caribbean slavery is still being fought with no end in sight.

But the enslavers monuments are being destroyed, one by one and more and more of the crimes of our Black, slavery, colonial history are being revealed to educate Black and White people globally of the wrongs, so they can be put right. This, I believe is the only way we will ever end racism.

The World Conference Against Racism was a bright light along our path and a lifeline onto which we can still hold firmly today and take more and more strong steps.

Let us press on, brave soldiers, let us press on!

We SHALL overcome!

ONE LOVE!

REPARATIONS

Coming home after the WCAR, I set up an online website on Reparations connecting those of us and the organizations who had been at WCAR. In time I built this into the Jamaica Reparations Movement, J.A.R.M., an online group of international Caribbean and Americans activists, including such members as as Ras Iral Jabari, Charles Ogletree and Randall Robinson, using the website and email to try and build the movement for Reparations in Jamaica.

This becan my intensive unpaid work to generate interest in the matter of Reparations, whose just cause had been endorsed by the United Nations in Durban. As well as the website, I spent my time writing articles, Letters to the Editor, making calls and giving interviews to journalists and radio stations. My most important action was creation of a Petition seeking signatures for the call for Reparations that I carried around with me to where people who should be interested in supporting Reparations were expected to be.

To my surprise, there was little support, especially not from those I thought would have stepped forward in strong numbers, especially the Rastafari community. I know that in their hearts they all supported Reparations, especially as a fund for Repatriation.

But they didn't come forward with verbal and personal support for either of the two public events I organized, or the many letters and articles I wrote in the local newspapers and online. Certainly no financial support.

The only money I ever got for my work on Reparations was from Lord Anthony Gifford, the White English lawyer and defender of both reparations and ganja legalizaton, who saw me one day waiting for a bus and offered me a ride. When I told him I had been delivering an article to the GLEANER on Reparations, he gave me Five Thousand Dollars, a huge amount of money in those days.

Other than that, I was on my own. All my work on Reparations came out of my very small pocket. I wasn't expecting payment, I didn't even see the financial possibility of the colonizing nations ever paying for slavery. But I didn't expect to be the only person doing the work. I was sure everyone was an enthusiastic about the topic, as I.

One person who gave help was Verene Shepherd, then Professor of History at the University of the West Indies, who invited me to speak on Reparations to a class of her students. I asked her to arrange in return for me to give a lecture at UWI and she did, arranging for me to use the Neville Hall Lecture Theatre to host an event in 2003.

I put out a public invitation and made some special invitations. Most important of all, I created a Reparations Document, an 8-page brochure featuring a full explanation of a proper Jamaican claim for Reparations. It included a Solemn Declaration, the Fundamental Objectives, the Forms of

Reparations, Structural Proposals, and the Plan of Action, all creating the Public Statement of Jamaica's Claims for Reprations.

About 30 people came, including my great friend Pearnel Charles, the MP, who had just been honoured as an African Chief. He brought with him fellow MP Mike Henry, who had recently proposed a Parliamentary debate on ganja legalization. Pearnel told Mike Henry to add Reparations to his debate and take them both to Parliament, which he did months later, beginning his ongoing support of Reparations.

Approved by the 30 persons gathered, the J.A.R.M Reparations Document became the historic foundation of the Government of Jamaica's decision to officially take Parliamentary action for Reparations. The brochure was quite an achievement to have finally put Jamaica's claim in writing and to have it approved by so many people from so many different sources. Rastas of differing Mansions, Garveyite Sister Mariam Samaad, poets, teachers, students, writers and Jamaicans. I was proud.

In 2004 I published an article giving a 'Rastafari Invoice for Repatriation with Reparations' issued by the J.A.R.M. that gained international publicity

While working with then-Minister of Culture Babsy Grange in 2007, the matter of Reparations came on her agenda and I submitted the J.A.R.M. Document to her as the basis of what could be proposed by Jamaica. She approved it and asked me to recommend a list of persons to set up a Parliamentary Committee chaired by Prof. Barry Chevannes to discuss the way forward on Reparations, based on the J.A.R.M.'s proposals. My first person I recommended was Prof. Verene Shepherd, who had been such an important help to me when I held the important J.A.R.M. Meeting. She proved to be the right person and has continued taking forward the struggle for Reparations since that appointment. The Committee's recommendations were accepted and then moved forward to a Parliamentary Debate led by MP Mike Henry where Reparations was finally accepted and approved.

    I was praised in the Debate by 4 MPs for the work of the J.A.R.M. and I was satisfied that all my hard work had an appropriate result. It was good to see action that would continue the work that was started in Durban.

    The work continues today through the setting up of a National Comission on Reparations and I am glad to have played a major role in making Jamaica's claim become stronger. Europe needs constant reminders of the evil they did and its after-effects. Only their humble apology and genuine acknowledgement of how their evil enabled them to enrich their nations, can end the perpetual racism built on the attitude of White Superiority over the Black race, that was practised with such horror and brutality in chattel slavery.

    But frankly, I don't think we will ever get Reparations – certainly not in the way Rastafari envisages it, namely as a big lump sum to pay for Repatriation to Africa for those who desire it, and their Resettlement. Those now heading the Reparations movement ask for other forms of payment like health care and education, or funding from foundations, corporations and universities donated by those that recognize their guilt and debt. But payment for Repatriation is not mentioned often.

What has not come is an apology from the many countries, organizations and families that benefited from slavery. Without that, nothing has changed except wider recognition of the debt due and the negative results of slavery that still remain. Those from whom an apology must come have perfected the act of never giving one.

What must come, instead, is an acknowledgement of the evils of White Supremacy, and an elevation of the ideals of Black Supremacy on which we have built a new world on the ashes we have inherited, without looking back, only forward. The Black Lives Matter movement is here at the right time to start setting that business right.

I no longer work for Reparations. To me, it's a waste of time because if any European nation was to truly pay the debt of slavery, it would bankrupt their nation out of existence. They see this even more clearly than I can, and European governments know their people will vote them out of power if they agree to pay Black people any large sum of Reparations out of their taxes.

A friend said I should apply to Thames Television for reparations to repay me for the income I lost when their bowing to racism caused me to lose the job and potential income. But 50 years later I see how many doors have been opened for Black British journalists, who ignore the block and kick the door open wider because I already did it as their example. When they praise me as a 'pioneer', a 'role model' and a 'living legend', for opening the door for them, I realise in the end I got the best reward and I smile to see lemonade made out of lemons. There is no reason for me to look back.

In the same way, perhaps instead of looking back at the very bad history that brought us to today, we could spend our energies looking at how much better we are now years later than our former colonizers. With all the money they have, their societies are a nightmare of crime, racism, child abuse, poor health, race wars, bad weather ... I could go on.

Meantime, Jamaica is envied as the most wonderful place on earth to be. Great music, great beaches, great mountains, great food, great sportsmen, great people. Everyone wants to be in Jamaica, people even wish they were Jamaicans. If only we knew how great Jamaica is, we would spend all our time building up our beautiful country to become a showplace, a living theme park and an example to the world that would end all the crime that is born in poverty.

The murders would end when we learn LOVE instead of hate. That's the kind of Reparations we need, the repair of the beautiful island that was handed over in 1834 with no compensation to the people who built it, the people who hacked out its forests into farms and villages, made roads out of dirt tracks and river banks, who planted food to feed themsleves and built houses out of wattle and daub to live in, and who gave thanks at the end of their labours to relax and swim in the clean rivers and the warm seas on white sand beaches.

It's ours now, and it's not even started to be as beautiful in every way, as it could be.   Look at where we are coming from 250 years after the end of slavery, from absolutely nothing to a modern nation proud of the accomplishments over decades of history of our famous citizens - too many to name - and proud creators of a new world religion, a new music and a new lifestyle culture.

So much money has been spent on salaries, lawyers, seminars, conferences, air fares and more, paying people to look for Reparations. The search looks likely to continue for many more decades. Is it worth it?

Jamaican reparations were certainly due to the Rastafari survivors of the infamous Coral Gardens Incident, so while working as Cultural Liaison to Minister of Culture Babsy Grange, I advised her that it was time to offer an apology and provide reparatory funding to the survivors. I was glad to help her Government make this happen, and after two years of work and negotiations I was also able to get the Government to set up a home for the most needy Elders. More is still to come to repair that wrong.

Instead of looking backwards to slavery and those who enslaved us, I prefer to look forward to build a future, as the Emperor advised Ethiopians to do after the defeat of the Italians. He said there should be no recrimination, no revenge.

"Instead, we must put to the best use the rich heritage of our past for, in that way, and in that way alone can we live to the highest standard set by our forefathers. We hope the future

generations will realize the magnitude of sacrifices that were required to accomplish all the works, so that they may preserve it as gain.

"Africans have been reborn as free men. The blood that was shed and the sufferings that were endured, are today Africa's advocates for freedom and unity. The glories and advantages of freedom cannot be purchased with all the world's material wealth."

I don't need any Reparations.

TO DAMN WITH FAINT PRAISE

'To Damn with faint praise" is a phrase used to describe words that seem to praise lightly, but by giving incomplete and false information, become a criticism and a damnation, rather than a compliment.

I have been damned with faint praise in a chapter of a book being heavily promoted that alleges to present several biographies of tribute to leading Rastafari Elders, among whom I am included. The chapter claiming to be about me mostly praises my work as a homeschooling mother, but excludes most of the things I have done relating directly to Rastafari. It concludes by stating: "Whatever can be said about certain controversial things she has spoken and provocative positions she has taken over the years, …. she must be considered a very brilliant and brave sister of whom the Movement is better off for having her than not."

Offering this faint praise, the damning statement in the chapter states: "She became negatively notorious within the Movement for being the subject of a STAR newspaper headline entitled 'No More Rasta For I" which was printed after she cut off her dreadlocks at the time. However, everyone passes through moments of confusion and depression and as such, that isolated episode should not be used to quantify the contribution of the potential of that person. She subsequently re-grew her dreadlocks and continued living as a Rasta."

I have become infamous by that article and there are more people who have repeated what they say I said that was quoted in the headline, than have actually read the article.

Those who actually read the article that that was published in the SUNDAY GLEANER Magazine (not the STAR) in 1982 under the headline "No More Rasta", will know that the article was a criticism of the fact that so many so-called-Rastas were not living the righteous life we were supposed to be living. 'Rastas' were becoming known as domestic abusers, adulterers, thieves, absent baby fathers, Rend-a-Dreads and party-goers, instead of living the divine priestly life that had been the livity of the foundation Elders and the Emperor himself. Most shocking of all was that a leading Rasta had been imprisoned to serve a long sentence for Fraud. The movement was in a critical condition.

In the article expressing my disappointment at how some Rastas were behaving, I said I could not see myself fitting into the description of 'Rasta' due to all that was being done by those describing themselves as 'Rasta'. So many were just wearing locks, smoking ganja, ignoring the Ten Commandments, behaving as they wished and calling whatever they did "Rasta", but not living up to what Bro. Dougie Mack had taught me in 1972 a Rasta should be. He had said that to be 'RasTafari' was to be like the Emperor, to do and live just like he did in every way.

The Emperor was the Defender of the Ethiopian Orthodox faith and lived according to its Biblical teachings, so I asked the beloved Ethiopian Archbishop Yesehaq to baptize me so I could become an Ethiopian Orthodox Christian as the Emperor was and continue following his example.

"Call me no more 'Rasta',| I wrote. "Call me the same name as the Emperor. Call me an Ethiopian Orthodox Christian." That was what the article was about. But few read the article and those who did ignored the message, perhaps because it hit hard at them. Instead they repeated the headine every time my name was mentioned. Many still do.

The book criticizing me had even more inaccuracies. It said I cut off my dreadlocks, but I had no dreadlocks to cut off when I wrote the article. At that time, just like my first Rasta teachers Dougie Mack, Sam Clayton and Count Ossie, I did not have dreadlocks. I still combed out my hair, but I always covered my head completely according to the teaching that a righteous woman always wears a 'crown'. My head-wrap was my crown. (I have been covering my head daily from them until now, except for two years 1978-79 when I took a job as PR for the City of Kingston). I did not start growing dreadlocks until my son was born in 1985.

After the article was published, I simply continued living in the same way I had been living, knowing it was the way someone who had come to Ethiopian Orthodox Christianity through Rastafari should live.

The book chose to ignore everything else I had done. There was no mention of my work as an active Garveyite writing many newspaper articles from the 1970s on Marcus Garvey and Garveyism; no mention of my leading role in the unveiling of the

Garvey statue at the St. Anns Bay Parish Library, or the naming of the Courtleigh Hotel in Kingston as the Marcus Garvey Building – some of which work which led to the UNIA awarding me a Lifetime Achievement Award in 2018.

Nor was there any mention of my work on Reparations that began on my return from the 2001 UN World Conference Against Racism, when I founded the Jamaica Reparations Movement (JARM) and wrote newspaper articles, spoke on radio, traveled around the island seeking signatures on a Reparations Petition, and holding meetings trying to interest the public in supporting Reparations for Repatriation. At one of these meetings held at the University of the West Indies, I presented the JARM document outlining what I felt should be the principles of Jamaica's call for reparations. It was signed by 30 persons attending the meeting, including Garveyite Sister Marianane Samaad, UWI History Professor Verene Shepherd, Maroon Chieftainess Gloria MamaG Simms, and MPs Pearnel Charles and Mike Henry, who was directed by the committee to raise the matter of Reparations in Parliament – which he did and continues to do.

There is no mention of the fact that in 2007, working with the then-Minister of Culture Olivia 'Babsy' Grange, I gave the JARM Document and all related material to the Government, saying I was done with trying to get Reparations. She used it to establish the Parliamentary Commission on Reparations headed by Prof. Barry Chevannes, that led to the establishment of the National Council on Reparations that still exists today.

The book's chapter writes that 'She shrugged off the criticisms of her peers ... to enter the political arena ... and become the first Rasta to be appointed as a Senator." I consulted with no 'peers' at my selection, nor heard any crticisms. I just accepted the appointment with surprise at having been given such an honour. I did not 'enter politics' or join a political party, but was a politically Independent member of the Opposition Senators appointed by the Governor General in the historic 'One Party Government" of 1984, becoming the only Rastafari and the only woman on the Opposition side of the Senate.

The book could have mentioned my support for decades in writing and in person of the call to legalize ganja, beginning with serving on the first Legalize It committee in the 1970s that included the legendary Ras DaSilva, UWI Professor Dennis Forsythe, and lawyers Sandra Alcott and Lord Anthony Gifford. It could have mentioned that when the Dangerous Drugs Act was finally updated in 2015 to allow the development of a ganja industry, I was the first to call on Government to wipe the records of those with convictions for simple ganja use. There is no mention of the fact that my work in ganja has continued to today, where I have served for the past 5 years on the Board of the Cannabis Licensing Authority, in recognition of my work in this area of Rastafari life.

The book admits that I founded the Reggae Film Festival, but does not mention that the event was a 5-year showcase of films highlighting the role of Rastafari in the creation, growth and global spread of reggae music culture.

All of the above things the book does not mention, are some of the reasons why in 2018 the Government of Jamaica awarded me the Order of Distinction "for contribution to Public Service in the field of Culture and Cultural Heritage Preservation".

For a book that claims to present information on noted Rastafari Elders who created and built the Movement, the inaccuracies in the chapter about me make me question the accuracy of the other chapters about other Elders, and especially to ask why other significant influencers of the early years are not mentioned, while others are given prominence.

I looked in vain to find biographies of Douglas Mack, Sam Clayton and Philmore Alvaranga, three of the four Rastafari who were sent on the historic Mission to Africa and who were invited by Emperor Haile Selassie to spend time in Ethiopia, years before his visit to Jamaica. The book only gives the biography of the fourth member of the Mission, Mortimo Planno. I looked in vain for a biography of Brother Gad, founder of the Twelve Tribes of Israel mansion that expanded Rastafari to the middle and upper classes. Several others are missing, while I of less achievements and fame am included.

Without these stories, the book is not only incomplete. More than that, it shows readers that they cannot trust a publication that contains a personal effort by little-known persons to achieve notoriety by falsely criticizing me, without considering the effect that can be conveyed by inaccuracies wrapped up in a red-gold-and-green cover.

Some think they know me, but they only know what they think they know of me. The chapter in this book claiming to be about me only tries to diminish my actual accomplishments. I would have preferred to join those Elders left out of this book, rather than to be damned by the faint praise the authors add to their inaccuracies and omissions.

Fortunately, I can tell my own tale, and I have written the story of the RasTafari life I have lived since 1972 in the book GROWING UP – DAWTA OF JAH that tells the full truths of my life story, some of which I have mentioned here. Let all PRAISE be to the Most High JAH who has directed all I have done in my 50 years of praying to H.I.M.

The long life I have been blessed with shows I did the right thing in praising H.I.M. And still doing that up to today.

THE STORY OF MR. JONES - A Windrush Tale

- - - - - - - -

CHAPTER ONE - THE ARRIVAL

ONE DAY IN 1954 MR. OBIDIAH JONES LOOKED AROUND HIM at his small farm on the hillsides of Portland, on which he grew yam, corn and bananas. Each week Mr. Jones reaped what crops were ready and took them on the back of his donkey up and down eight miles of hillside to the market in Port Antonio.

Mr. Jones was tired of the hard life he lived. He had five children and a wife, and he was ashamed that no matter how hard he worked, his future would always be one of hard work, a constant search for money to pay for necessities like kerosene oil for the lamp and clothes for the children to go to the Government school nearby.

He had heard, as he talked with his friends in the rum shop at night, that many Jamaicans were selling their land and using the money to pay for a passage to England. England, his friends told him, was a place where all men had equal opportunity to work hard and get a good wage, a place where people were housed and fed and clothed and educated.

So Mr. Jones sold his land, sent his wife and children to live with her sister in Manchioneal, and took his money to a travel agent in Kingston, who assured him that he could secure the correct travel documents to enable him to go to England. Mr. Jones sailed to England on a ship named 'Windrush' in a cabin which he shared with five others like himself. The food on the ship was not very tasty, so he and his friends dug into the packages they had brought with them and ate the bananas, mackerel, honey and drank the rum to keep them warm as the nights grew colder.

The ship landed at a dock in a city names Liverpool. His first glimpse of England was a profound shock to him. Nowhere were the opulent buildings he had seen photographs of. Instead, he saw dirty streets, ugly houses with scabby faces, dirty children shouting at each other in a language he did not understand, and over everything, the thick grayness of fog and rain that was the English climate.

Everywhere, everyone around him was White. He had never seen so many White people at one time before in his life. In fact, he had only seen White people on the occasions when he went into Kingston on business, and even then, only one or two at a time.

The men who shared the cabin with Mr. Jones said they were going to take a train to London, where there were jobs and places to live. Mr. Jones collected his suitcases and joined them at the ticket counter, then on the train to London. When the train arrived, relatives met each of them, so Mr. Jones was alone in the strange city. He stopped the first Black man he saw and shyly asked him where he could find somewhere to stay for the night, until he found a place to live. The man directed him to an address in Notting Hill Gate and told him to take a Number 7 bus that would take him there.

Mr. Jones found the address was a large house, three stories high, with rooms on every floor. There was no landlord to answer Mr. Jones questions, but one man who lived there and seemed to be in charge told Mr. Jones that he was welcome to stay there, if he was prepared to share a bed. Sharing a bed, Mr. Jones discovered, meant two men sharing a bed in half-day shifts, Mr. Jones sleeping in the day while the other man worked through the night shift. In the morning when the man returned, Mr. Jones would have to vacate the bed and find a job to occupy himself in the daytime and earn enough to pay the rent.

Mr. Jones did not mind too much. He was more concerned with the cold. The paraffin fire in his room was turned down at night by the other lodger, who said that paraffin cost more than wearing all your clothes to bed. Mr. Jones thought he would never be warm again.

Each day he got dressed and went out looking for work. The other lodger had told him that work could be found if he inquired at the Labour Exchange, so each day Mr. Jones went to the Labour Exchange and sat on the benches, patiently waiting his turn to sit before the clerk and go through the list of jobs available.

The clerk had a thick index file of jobs, but it seemed that none of these jobs were available to Mr. Jones. He had no qualifications, the clerk told him. These jobs required a skill of some sort. There were some unskilled jobs in factories or offices, but the clerk would tell Mr. Jones that employers were only willing to hire White workers, since the other employees, or the factory boss, or the factory's neighbours, did not want to have coloured workers alongside them.

One day, his money running desperately low, Mr. Jones found a job sweeping up shavings in a furniture factory. It wasn't hard work, but Mr. Jones did not like it. He hated the shame of being the lowest worker. He hated the scorn with which the White workers regarded him. He hated the insults they spat at him: *"Gollywog!", "Coon!", "Nig Nog"*. *"Hey, Sambo*! Over here needs sweeping!" But he could do no better. He needed the work and the money.

When he walked home through the streets at night, he hung his head and hoped that by hunching up his shoulders and scuffling unobtrusively along the pavement, his colour, his shabbiness and his shame would not be too noticeable.

At night in his room he composed letters to his family telling them that he was doing well, working in a factory, taking home a regular pay check – some of which he was enclosing in the form of a Postal Order. Then he would eat the fish and chips he had bought on the way home, turn down the paraffin heater and set his alarm for 5 the next morning, so he could get up, get ready and get out before the night shift worker needed the bed.

On Saturdays and Sundays Mr. Jones would try to find a place to live. He looked at the advertisements in the papers and in the windows of the newspaper shops and would write down the more promising addresses. But after a few weeks of doing that, Mr. Jones grew discouraged with hearing the same excuses every time. The flat had just been let ... the landlord had changed his mind about letting it ... they preferred a married couple. One day a woman came right out and said that yes, the flat was for rent, but not to Niggers.

    Eventually Mr. Jones found a room, quite by accident, in the house of a middle-aged Welsh woman, Mrs. Davies. Mrs. Davies had no prejudices and loved to cook. She had two grown children, a boy and a girl, who on their occasional visits would ignore Mr. Jones. He learned to be out whenever the children came to visit.

    One night, feeling the need for female company, Mr. Jones went to a club. The only Black women there, Mr. Jones could see from the way they behaved and dressed, were prostitutes. He could not bring himself to speak to them. There were some White women in the club, although there were no White men. One of them came over and sat beside Mr. Jones. She wasn't pretty, but she talked with him about Jamaica, which she had heard about from her last boyfriend – a Jamaican who she said used to beat her, and left her pregnant. Mr. Jones invited her to come back and have some coffee with him.

    On the way home, walking through the dark, dank streets, four White men stepped out from behind a wall and beat up Mr. Jones. They told him that Niggers should stick to their own kind, instead of soiling White women, and that if they ever saw him again with a White women, they would kill him. Mr. Jones believed them.

The time had come, Mr. Jones realized, to send for his woman. It took longer than he had thought, because Mr. Jones was not married to his woman, and in England people did not understand about common-law wives. But two years later, Mr. Jones' woman arrived. The first thing they did was to get married.

Mrs. Davies was happy to have another woman in the house. Mr. Jones was happy too. He had worked his way up in the factory to the assembly line and, by doing overtime at nights and on Sundays, he could almost double his pay packet.

The overtime money, he saved to send for his youngest child, who was glad to escape the brutality of grand-motherly care in Jamaica. Meanwhile, Mrs. Jones had two more children. After the first one, she vowed she wouldn't have any more, because while in the hospital the nurses and other patients abused her, saying that all Black women did was breed. But by the time she was pregnant with the second child, she too had grown used to insulting remarks.

In between children, Mrs. Jones worked as a conductress on the No.7 bus route, which ran from Notting Hill through the

West End of London to the tough-war-scarred East End. Mrs. Jones reckoned that she heard more insults and abuse daily, than her husband.

Just before the birth of the second child, Mrs. Davies told the Joneses that the Council had placed a demolition order on her house. Mr. Jones had noticed that many of the houses in the street had been vacated and boarded up, but he had just thought that was because the houses had finally rotted down, which they looked like they were going to when he first moved in. After all, Mrs. Davies' house had only a kitchen sink for washing in, and an outside lavatory behind the house in the yard.

Mrs. Davies explained to them that the area was scheduled for re-development. That meant that the local Council would be pulling down all the houses and rebuilding a brand new housing estate which would be ready in about five years time. Because she had lived there for eleven years, Mrs. Davies would be immediately rehoused in another Council estate in the suburbs of London. Mrs. Davies was pleased.

Mr. Jones wasn't, because he knew that this meant that he and his family would have to look for somewhere else to live. It took him almost a year to find a place and when he did, it wasn't in the green open suburbs near his factory, as he wished, but just two streets away. He was still in Notting Hill.

This house wasn't like Mrs. Davies'. On the floor below lived a White prostitute and her Black man. At night Mr. and Mrs. Jones were kept awake by the noises of footsteps on the stairs, doors being slammed, drunks shouting, music playing and, occasionally, the sound of the woman being beaten up by her man.

Above them lived an old White woman, a relative of the landlord, who banged her stick on the floor whenever the children cried or made the usual noises of children growing up. They dared not answer her back, because they knew that she would complain to the landlord, who would give them notice to leave. So they suffered in silence, beating the children to keep them quiet.

When Mr. Jones had saved up enough money to send for the youngest child, the boy was seven and could not read or write. Mrs. Jones was glad when her son arrived, because now she would have someone to look after the babies each day, instead of having to take them to the baby-minder. She had never liked sending them to the baby minder, who lived in a large, damp basement into which she herded twenty children each day, changing their diapers and wiping their noses whenever she could spare a minute from her job of cooking chicken and rice-and-peas lunch for the neighbourhood Jamaicans.

With a third child to house. Mr and Mrs Jones moved their bed into the living room, giving the children the single bed and a cot to sleep on in the bedroom. It didn't matter that they slept in the living room, since they had no visitors. One night, in the cold winter of 1962 when the pipes froze solid and the cold came through the walls in the form of water, Mrs. Jones left the paraffin stove burning in the children's room.

Luckily, Mrs. Jones woke up and smelled smoke, or else the children would have burned up just like the old stuffed chair beside the stove had gone up in flames.

The landlord was very angry, but fortunately the prostitute's boyfriend who was out of jail at the time, spoke to the landlord on their behalf. He spoke to the landlord very loudly, and Mr. Jones thought he heard the boyfriend threatening the landlord, but he couldn't be sure. After that, Mr. Jones did not care what business the boyfriend was in, he was so grateful to have found one person in the whole of England who cared about him and his family.

CHAPTER TWO - GEORGE

The propstitute's name was Margot. It was her real name, though no one believed her, especially not the two young men who offered her a ride as she stood at Euston Station that first morning, wondering what to do now that she had finally arrived in London.

She had come south with the intention of going to secretarial school and using her prominent breasts to advance her career where her intelligence, she knew, would fail her. So when they had said to her "Looking for someone, luv?" she had tossed her head and giggled and said "Not specially," and they had said "Well, let's share a taxi," and she had thought, why not.

Margot hadn't cared that the two boys were Black. She had always wanted to be chatted up by a Black boy, only her mother in Liverpool would have killed her if she had caught her speaking to one. Mum didn't like Blacks.

Margot didn't see why not. They always wore nice clothes and smiled at her, and her girlfriends said they had big cocks. That had interested Margot. Big cocks meant big satisfaction, satisfaction which she hadn't got standing up in smelly alleys hoping none of her friends would see her late Saturday nights coming home from the pictures with one of the dockside boys.

These two seemed like perfect gentlemen. They hadn't mentioned her tits, like all the White boys did first time they spoke to her. "Lovely tits you've got, Margot, give us a feel," they would say and grab at her with dirty-fingernailed hands. The one sitting beside her on the left, the one who said his name was George, was looking at her tits all during the ride, though.

"Come up for the shopping, have you?" the one called Roy asked.

"No. Come up to live. I'm going to be a secretary. I'm going to find a flat in the West End and buy myself some pretty clothes first, though."

George had said nothing during the ride, apart from telling her his name. Roy did all the talking. Roy said that they had a flat in the West End, if she wanted to stay for a while until she found a place. Margot had heard of sharing with guys, but she thought she'd have to wait and see. These two seemed alright enough, but they were only the first two men she had met in London. There must be hundreds like them and hundreds better. She'd wait and see.

They had gotten out of the cab in a very unimpressive street. Not much better than the street she had lived on in Liverpool, Margot thought. But inside the flat, Margot was in heaven. She had never been in such a nice place before. It was dark inside with black curtains over the windows and the place was lit by several lamps, some with red and gold bulbs, some with figurines of gnomes and dancing ladies.

Over one window was a string of Christmas lights. There was a shaggy goatskin rug on the floor on which Margot wanted to put her bare feet, only she didn't want to take off her shoes and expose the hole in the toe of her tights. The sofa was a bed really, covered with an imitation leopard skin rug and lots of little cushions. There was a very elaborate record player in a corner, connected by lots of wires to two speakers – much nicer than the portable one she and her girlfriend used to play 45s on in the basement beside the church back in Liverpool – and a TV set.

There were lots of pictures on the walls, pictures of mountains sceneries, a picture of a Chinese-looking woman, a poster of a bullfighter and another poster with the word JAMAICA on it. There was a picture of a man who was playing three horns at once, and another picture of a Black man who seemed to be a priest or something.

Roy had opened a cupboard and Margot could glimpse inside lots of bottles of drink, not just cheap wine, but Scotch and gin and other things. And when he asked her what she wanted to drink, Margot had said "gin and it" even though she didn't know what "it" was other than something she used to hear women call for as she sipped a glass of beer in the pub on Saturday nights.

Well, you couldn't ask for a pale ale here, Margot thought. Roy had laughed and given her a gin with something pinky looking in it, but it had tasted nice and she was glad that she had accepted their offer to ride with them in the taxi.

When they had suggested that she have a bath and change her clothes and come out shopping with them, Margot hadn't looked in the least surprised that they should want her to bathe when it wasn't Saturday night. She was glad she hadn't refused, because the bathroom was almost as nice as the living room. It had a bathtub and a basin and a piece of carpet over the linoleum floor, and there was hot water which Roy turned on from a white box on the wall over the bath. He even put some powder in the water, which made it smell ever so nice.

She hated getting out of the bath, it was so nice, but the water was getting cold, so she put a towel around her and put her head around the door and asked where her things were. George, who was the only one in the living room, just pointed at a door which Margot realized was the bedroom. Does he never speak, Margot thought huffily, as she went into the bedroom.

And surprise, surprise! Guess who's lying on the bed, naked as all creation and smiling too, but Roy! Well, why not, thought Margot as she removed the towel and let him look at her breasts. Bet they don't see much of that now.

Roy didn't stop laughing while they screwed. Margot didn't laugh much, she was so surprised. This was much better than she had ever had. Wait till she told her friends in Liverpool. Bet they'd want to know if was true about Black men's cocks. Well it was, but she wouldn't tell them. At least, not right away. She'd let them beg her first. Then she'd brag about it, and about how long he was at it. Yes, this was much better, soft and tender and if she shut her eyes, she could almost imagine that he was White and like the man she used to think about when she put her hands between her legs alone in the bed on cold Liverpool nights.

She was lying there thinking how lucky she was, getting off the train and finding a boyfriend right away, and finding such a nice flat to live in, when George put his head around the door and said "Ready?" in a very bored voice, and then closed the door.

Roy got up and had a bath and then shaved and put on some nice smelling lotion on his face and body, and put on clean clothes – such nice clothes, all bright and fashionable. Margot was glad she had packed her pink wool mini and green sweater that showed off her tits.

They had taken another taxi to Oxford Street, which she had heard so much about and which was ten times better than she had ever dreamed, full of people carrying packages, cars waiting in the traffic, store windows jam packed with all sorts of things she wanted to own.

"Look at that watch! Oh, isn't that a lovely dress – just my colour! And those shoes!"

Margot realized that she needed so many clothes, if she was to look as smart as the girls she passed in the street. A lot of people stared at her and maybe it was because her clothes weren't fashionable, but then maybe it was because they were just jealous of her being with two such good looking men. She wondered if they could tell which one of them was screwing her, or if they thought both of them were.

They went into a shoe shop and Roy helped her choose a lovely pair of white shoes. George paid for them and he seemed to have such a lot of money in his wallet. She was glad they were rich too. Maybe she wouldn't have to work after all, just stay home and dust the place and wait for Roy to come home from work each evening.

They went to a club that night near Paddington Station, full of Black men and girls and some White girls, and lots of throbbing Black music that Margot hadn't heard before. Everyone danced so well, that Margot knew she was going to have to learn all the new steps, and when the Black men came and asked her dance Margot thought now was as good a time as any to start learning.

The men held her close and pressed their legs between hers so she could feel their cocks hard on her thigh, but Roy had been watching and he didn't seem to mind at all, so she just let them. These Black people do things different. A Liverpool boy would have killed any man who asked his date to dance – let alone dance like THAT.

George didn't dance, though, and Margot wished he would even dance with her. What was the matter with him? Was he queer or something? Or was he just jealous? He hardly seemed to notice her, even though she spoke to him just as much as to Roy. He didn't even seem to have a girlfriend. Maybe his girl had just left him and he was sad about it.

Margot thought she would try and cheer him up. She told him about Liverpool and her Mum who had called her Margot after the ballet dancer, and her father who worked on the docks and drank a lot, and how her mother was always crying at night, and how sometimes her father would beat up her mother and then they wouldn't see him for days.

Her father loved her though, Margot told George, a bit too much her Mam used to say, but Margot didn't mind. When her father had died one day, an industrial accident they called it, Margot had cried for weeks. Her mother used to hit her when she found Margot crying, and then she used to hit Margot more often when Margot started going out with boys.

"You're no better than a whore," she used to scream at Margot. But Margot just used to push out her chin and say, "Well if I was a whore, I'd be living in luxury instead of this stinking hole" and comb her hair again before she slammed the door behind her.

At nights Margot and Roy and George would go out to a club and dance, and people would come over to their table and talk. Some evenings they would just sit in the flat with the lights turned on and some Black music on the record player, and more friends would come over and they would all sit and talk. Most of the time Margot didn't understand what they were saying, they talked so funny – not like the Blacks in Liverpool did, but like they weren't talking English at all.

Margot liked those evenings when friends came over, for all she would have to do was make drinks and she would get a chance to wear her new clothes and they didn't mind if she sat and did her nails with the new polish she had bought that day. And when the friends left, she and Roy would go to bed and screw. She was always glad to be in bed with Roy, because every time he found some new way to screw. He never did it the same way twice, always different.

She wondered if George knew different ways too, other than the ways Roy did it. She had got used to George now, and she got used to Roy never answering her questions about George. In fact, he never answered her questions about where they worked, or how they always had so much money, or where they went some evenings they left her alone. But she didn't mind. Life was nice.

One day Roy told her he wanted her to do a favour for a friend.

"What sort of favour?" she asked.

"He'll tell you," was all Roy said.

Later that evening he came back home with a Black man. He told Margot to give him a drink and while Margot was pouring it, he said he'd soon be back.

Margot didn't know what to say to the man. He wasn't one of the friends she had met before, she was sure of that, and he didn't way much except to answer Margot's questions about whether it was still raining, or if he had come far. But he seemed quite nice and quite handsome too, and after a while Margot saw him looking at her tits and he smiled at her and gestured his head towards the bedroom, and Margot thought: "Well if I'm quick I'll find out if they all do it different".

He hadn't done it different. In fact, he was very much like the boys in Liverpool – wham, bam, thank you mam – but at least now she knew. When he was finished, he just put on his clothes and left, and not a minute too soon because no sooner than she heard the front door slam, she heard Roy coming up the stairs.

"Your friend just left," Margot said.

"Yes I saw him going," Roy said.

"What was the favour you wanted me to do for him?" Margot asked.

But all Roy said to her was "Go take a bath" as if he knew that she really needed a bath after what she'd just done.

A couple of days later Roy said he had another favour he wanted her to do. This time, when the man looked towards the bedroom, Margot suddenly knew what the favour was, but it was such a giggle. Roy's friends were hard up for a screw and so Roy had loaned her to them. She'd heard once that when you visit an Eskimo, he offers you his wife as a token of his hospitality. Margot assumed that Blacks were more or less the same. After all, Roy didn't seem to mind. He still smiled all the time, so it must be quite normal to him.

The third time Roy asked her to do him a favour, she had giggled and said "Who is it this time?" But he hadn't answered. Instead he had gone out. Sometime later, George knocked at the door. There was a White man with him.

"Roy's out," Margot said.

"I know," George said. "This is a friend of his." And he had pushed the man through the door and closed it behind him.

Margot was so astonished. And a bit ashamed. What would a White man think of her, living her with a Black man? She wondered if he was from Liverpool and knew her Mam and would go back and tell her he had seen Margot. But he spoke, and Margot could tell he wasn't from Liverpool at all. In fact, he had a very nice accent, sort of upper class, Margot thought.

But she didn't like him at all. He was old, at least 40, and his hair was thin and stuck to his head, and his hands were fat with short fingers. Margot remembered a girlfriend saying that you could tell how big a man's cock was from the size of his thumb, and this man had short thumbs.

God no, Margot thought. He doesn't expect THAT kind of favour, does he? She couldn't. She just couldn't.

"Well little miss, let's get on with it, shall we?" he had said and reached across to grab her breast.

"How dare you touch me!" Margot had said and jumped up from the sofa.

"Come on, let's not play games," he said. "Half an hour is all I've got."

"Half an hour! For what?" Margot was aghast.

"Come, little Miss Innocent. Or do you want to put on a veil and play Virgin Bride?" And he stood up and advanced towards Margot, holding out his arms.

Margot pushed him and he fell, and as he hit the floor he swore.

"Bitch! Who the fuck do you think you are? I've already paid for this. I'll beat the shit out of you, and Blackie too, I warn you!"

Margot screamed, and then a lot of things happened at once. The door had opened and George had come in and the man had hit George and George had hit him and given him a bloody nose and pushed him out the door.

And then George had hit her, slapped her so hard she had fallen on the sofa, and then he was punching her hard, in the face, on her breasts, in her back, kicking her when she fell on the floor, hitting her again when she tried to get up, calling her 'whore' and saying where the fuck did she think all the money came from – heaven?

And that she had better start paying her way or he would beat her so badly, he'd kill her, or that he would cut up her face so bad that no man would want to look at her again, and that she had better learn fast to be nice to their friends, and if she ever thought of running away his friends would find her and kill her.

And finally when Margot sobbed on the floor, holding her face and hoping that her tooth wasn't going to fall out and leave a hole in the front of her face, he had pushed up her dress and torn down her panties and screwed her right there on the floor.

And even though she was in pain all over, it was so sweet, the sweetest ever, so sweet that right at THAT moment, with her eyes closed tightly and tears rolling down her face, she had cried out "Daddy!"

CHAPTER THREE - THE CHILDREN

They became friends, Mr. Jones and the Boyfriend, whose name was George. Sometimes when the prostitute was out working, George would invite Mr. Jones down to his flat. Mr. Jones would sit there, sipping George's whiskey, surrounded by such luxuries as a television set, hi-fi, carpet instead of linoleum, while George would tell him stories of his escapades, his stints in prison, his constant plans to outwit the law, and always, his hatred of White people.

Mr. Jones couldn't understand how George could hate White people and yet live with a White women. George only laughed and told him that she was neither the first nor the only White woman he had. Mr. Jones felt grateful to George just for being a strong Black man friend.

One day George asked Mr. Jones to do him a favour. He wanted Mr. Jones to stand bail for him in court, because he knew no one he could ask who did not already have a prison record. Glad to do his friend a favour, Mr. Jones agreed and on the appointed day brushed off his one suit and his hat and went to the Marylebone Magistrates Court. Inside of himself, Mr. Jones was frightened. He had never been to court before and knew he would have to swear that he had known George a long time and that, should George skip bail, he would be responsible for payment.

George's crime was that he had stolen three T-shirts from a stall in Portobello Road. That was the official charge. But George told Mr. Jones that he never stole a T-shirt in his life. He said the truth was that the Police knew that George knew the name of a Jamaican who had killed a policeman and if George was to tell them where to find that man, he would get off the charge.

When they got to court, the Police took George into the cells and when they came back out and into court, the Policeman informed the Magistrate that he had overlooked a serious offense when making out the charge, that of carrying a dangerous weapon. The Magistrate said that in that case, the case would have to be remanded, so Mr. Jones stood bail and they left the courthouse.

Mr. Jones got to know George and his friends very well. After a while he got used to having to step out into the street if he was there when George's woman came back with a customer. At those times they would walk down to the Jamaican restaurant that sold Stew Peas and patties late into the night, and talk with George's friends.

He met Maxie, the bus driver who used to play cricket in St. Elizabeth. He met Leroy, the brown-skinned engineering student who lived on an allowance from his parents and came to see George whenever he needed ganja to smoke. He met Prince, who had the record shop on All Saints Road. He met Carl, who had the bookshop selling revolutionary pamphlets where they used to perform Black plays on Saturday nights.

Mr. Jones thought they were all very mad. He couldn't understand why they all didn't settle down and get a good job, and learn to live in peace with the English man, like he was doing.

Mr. Jones didn't like being at home much nowadays. The children were now going to school and he didn't know what to say to them when they came home at nights with sad faces and stories of being called *'Nigger'* and *'Sambo'* and being spat on at school. His eldest son was always getting into fights at school. He didn't know what to say to them, so he would just tell them to study and get an education, because a man could go anywhere with an education.

There was a youth club in the neighbourhood. Mr. Jones had gone there once with his eldest son and he was pleased to see racial integration at work, White and Black children playing ping pong, dominoes and records under the watchful eye of the priest from All Saints Church. But then he began to hear stories of fights breaking out on the street when the children were going home after the club closed, and then complains from neighbours about the noise.

One night he heard police sirens, and when his son didn't come home and his wife was getting frantic, he put on his hat and coat and went down to the Police station to find his son and several other Black youths in cells there. There had been a fight, the Police said. They were closing down the youth club, the Police said.

When he got him out of the station and back home, Mr. Jones beat his son that night. He didn't care about the old lady upstairs that night. No member of his family had ever got into trouble before. It was no use Mr. Jones' son telling him that he was only defending himself against racist skinheads. Mr. Jones was ashamed. What sort of example was his son setting for his younger sister and brother? The girl was wild enough, and she was only ten. They had all better change their ways now, before it was too late.

George's case came up again and was postponed. And again it came up. Each time Mr. Jones went to court and stood bail.

One evening his wife told him that he teacher had come around that day after school and told her that the youngest son would have to be put in a special school, a school called "ESN". Mr. Jones didn't know what that meant, so he asked George next day. George told him that it was a school for Educationally Sub-Normal children.

Mr. Jones was ashamed again. He thought it was his fault that his child was backward, since he had never been to school himself. He blamed himself, and when the day came to send his youngest son to the special school, he cried all the way on the bus, the tears rolling down his cheeks silently while he held his son's hand.

The school was pretty and bright with lots of toys and smiling young teachers. He was glad that his son didn't look like some of the other children, with swollen heads, dribbling mouths, pulling themselves across the floor, or huddled in a corner whimpering. That night Mr. Jones went for a long walk, and thought a lot.

A few weeks later, Mr. Jones had a good laugh. He read in the newspaper that a Black political party calling itself RAAS had been formed by a Trinidadian named Michael X. He thought it must be a joke, because every Jamaican knew that RAAS was the baddest word in the language. But when he kept reading about the man week after week, he asked George about him.

George told him it was a joke, but not a joke. He said that he knew the man, because they used to work together one time as strong-arm men evicting Black people out of houses when they wouldn't or couldn't pay the rent. He said the man used to run women too, like George did, and had been in jail a few times too, like George. Mr. Jones was not pleased. He wondered why people were taking this Michael X seriously and why the Black people had not told the papers he did not represent them.

Mr. Jones soon had more to worry about. He read in his paper that a politician named Enoch Powell had said that Britain should not allow any more Black people into the country, or else there would be another race riot.

Mr. Jones remembered the first race riots. He had stayed indoors the whole time, afraid to walk on the street because he had heard of the White gangs roaming around looking for Black people to beat up. He had peeped out from his window once and seen a group of Black women going shopping, walking in the center of a group of Black men armed with bottles and sticks to protect them. He had been very frightened.

After the riots, when he heard that several men had been arrested, he had been glad, but then he read that the men were all Black and Mr. Jones had been puzzled as to why only Black men had been arrested.

Now Mr. Jones was frightened in the same way. Mr. Jones wondered why it was that people did not want him and people like him to be happy. All he wanted was to live peacefully and earn a living. He wasn't taking work from anyone. He had read somewhere that Black people were only two percent of the population of Britain, and that they were necessary if the buses and hospitals and postal services were to operate.

Moreover, he remembered that Jamaica paid taxes in one form or other to England, and that England owned Jamaica from 1655 till quite recently when Jamaica became Independent in 1962. So why did they mind if he came and lived in England for a little while?

Things began to get worse for Mr. Jones. People started abusing him on the street loudly now. Mrs. Jones quit her job as a bus conductress, because the abuse she was getting made her afraid. When Mr. Jones watched television in George's flat, every night there was something new about Enoch Powell, what he had said that day, how much support he had in the country, and how it was time to stop Black immigration.

They put George in prison one day. Mr. Jones was alone again. Mrs. Jones wasn't much company. She used to cry at night because she missed her youngest son. Her eldest son never came home at night nowadays. Instead, he slept on a mattress at another youth club and only came home in the days to eat, bathe and change when Mr. Jones was at work. Mr. Jones had never been to that club, but heard that only Black people were allowed in it, and that the young people who went there were 'undesirable'.

Mr. Jones eldest son came home one night, though. He came home with a girl and told Mr. Jones that he was getting married. The girl was White and not very clean. Mrs. Jones did not like her. Mr. Jones did not know what to think. Perhaps his son would be better off with a White wife. Perhaps people would accept his son then, even if they did not accept him. But Mr. Jones was not happy. After all, they were only seventeen years old, even though the girl looked older. What would happen to their children, he wondered, when they grew up neither Black nor White?

The girl told Mr. Jones that she already had one brown child. Mr. Jones got angry with his son. He told him the girl was no better than a whore and that if she was the best he could do, then he never wanted to see his eldest son again. He hit his eldest in the face when he answered him back.

Later that night, Mr. Jones went for another long walk and thought a lot more. Perhaps it was time to go back home to Jamaica. Things must be getting better there, because every now and then he would read something about Jamaica in the paper, something good. He knew that he no longer had any land to go back to, but surely there must be a furniture factory somewhere in Jamaica that had room for someone with as much experience of English furniture manufacturing as he had gained in his years sweeping up and doing odd jobs at the factory.

Mr. Jones took a day off from work and traveled to the office of the Jamaican High Commission. It was a big, beautiful office down in the rich part of London, and inside it was cool and bright with pictures of Jamaican Prime Ministers and Heroes and beaches and flowers. A nicely dressed young lady called Mr. Jones into her office, smiling with him as she talked. She told him that Jamaica now had a large furniture industry, and she gave him the addresses so he could write them and ask for a job.

She said the Government could not pay his passage back to Jamaica. But she said that Jamaica needed skilled people to "come home and contribute". Mr. Jones did not know what the lady meant by "contribute", but he went home and talked about it with his wife and his daughter.

His wife was surprised, but happy at the thought of leaving England. Mrs. Jones had had enough. She missed the blue skies of Jamaica, the constant sunshine, the green of the leaves, the souond of the trickle of a small river, the smell of rain on the earth. She wanted her children to grow up in that country, with those sights and sounds and smells.

But Mrs. Jones daughter said she did not want to leave her friends in England. She said she heard that Jamaica was poor, people lived in trees and there was no television.

Mr. and Mrs. Jones decided to start saving for their fare back to Jamaica. They know their retirement Pension will help them build a house when they get back home.

CHAPTER FOUR - GEORGE'S STORY

Allman Town, Kingston was never a nice place to live, certainly not in 1958 when George, second eldest of Miss Tinson's five boys (she who sold fry fish in the glass box at street corner every Thursday and Friday night), found himself in an uncomfortable position with the Police. They wanted to speak to him regarding a watch belonging to a certain United States sailor who, before departing after his ship's shore leave, had reported it stolen by two boys who had led him to an assignation with a prostitute in Rae Town, also in Kingston.

The police also wanted to speak to George about a number of similar incidents, and George knew that it was no use explaining to the Police that the sailor, like many other of his wise-guy comrades before him, had tried to have his pleasure without paying, and had to have the situation explained to him with polite force. No, George didn't think they would understand, especially since the constable leading the search also wanted to speak to George about a private matter concerning a certain girl who professed to be the policeman's sweetheart, but whom George had lured away with talk of love.

So he checked his friend on the wharf, who he knew had helped a friend of his in a similar position to get on to a ship going to England, and one sunny morning he walked up to the ship's side with a hat on his head, Fifty Pounds in his pocket, but otherwise empty hands and, in a pre-arranged strategy, gave a shout and a wave to a man standing dockside, who signaled him to come like a long lost friend.

"Just going to have a word with me frien'," George explained to the guard, who was relaxedly watching the comings and goings on and off the ship, which wasn't due to sail for another day. Pretending long-lost friendship, George and his newfound friend had a few drinks at the bar, sitting and talking about cricket and local gossip until the sun started lowering its fiery orb into the sea behind them. Then, when no one was noticing, his friend walked George to a special hiding place and told him to stay there as long as he could.

George fell asleep, but soon his cramped position and full bladder made life unbearable. He felt the ship sail and his fears diminished a little, but his adrenalin was pumping all the time. Two days later, and not a moment too soon, George heard a tap at his hiding place and there stood his friend and another man. They took him to a small cabin in the depths of the ship, where George paid them Twenty Pounds each and had his first meal from the second man's bundles of fried fish, potato pudding, fried dumplings and white rum.

The ship was one of the many Italian ships which had cornered the market in transporting Jamaicans to Britain and thereby created the newest Middle Passage, which differed from the first only in that the slaves paid their own fares, since the conditions of travel were not much different from the original slave barges.

By the time the weather grew colder and the calm of the Caribbean Sea was replaced by the rough Atlantic Ocean, George's fear had vanished, to be replaced with the furtiveness of a rat, whose cunning he realized he would have to adopt to survive in the unknown world he was about to enter illegally, armed only with the fake passport for which he had paid Fifty Pounds to a man in downtown Kingston.

When the ship landed in Liverpool, George, visibly relieved at having passed undetected through Immigration accepted a kind invitation from a dockside cabbie to drive him to London, his destination, where he hoped to find Ricketts, another Allman Town boy who he heard had made it across like him. It was only after the taxi had been driving for more than an hour on open highway, that George thought of asking just how long a trip it would be.

"Six hours," the cabbie said over his shoulder.

Geezas, thought George. "How much is that going to cost?" he asked.

"Twenty-five Pounds," the cabbie replied, in a way that made George realize that he had been had.

"Stop the car," he yelled. "I feel sick."

And when the driver walked around to see what was the matter, George uncurled from his crouch position on the grassy bank and gave the cabbie a real Kingston beating, complete with threats of what he would do to the cabbie if the cabbie didn't take him to London for free, damn cheating raass. He showed the driver the knife he had stolen on the ship and sharpened in the hours of travel.

Bawling with pain and humiliation, as well as fear of George perched with his knife on the seat beside him, the driver completed the trip, but refused to take George any closer than Paddington Station, where he threatened to call the Police on George.

George escaped into a group of Black men coming off duty as station attendants, who listened to his story and offered him temporary lodgings at the house where one of them lived. Using his Allman Town wits, George soon met up with men like himself, Ladbroke Grove residents who sold ganja and women and ran run-down clubs where West Indians could drink, gamble and pick up women.

Not for George the dreary grind of trying to find a job through the Labour Exchange. He had checked out that source of income and found that it was only after subjecting a person to a humiliatingly long wait and scrutiny, that the bald-headed White inquisitor behind the counter would condescendingly dole out a job which amounted to nothing more than being a street sweeper, the lowest factory hand, or to clean up the slops in a hospital. Even if George had a skilled trade such as carpentry or welding, he wouldn't have taken any of the miserable jobs which he saw Black tradesmen doing.

Soon George had a small reputation as a successful hustler. He threw his first dance, a raucous sound session in a second floor Westbourne Grove flat in which a prostitute he lived off, lived. Even though the police eventually raided just as the session was getting hot, George raised about Forty Pounds.

As if informed of George's success, Ricketts magically appeared and insisted that he and George go into partnership.

Looking at the three men who had accompanied Ricketts with his request, George used his discretion and accepted Ricketts offer. This was a new Ricketts: sharp clothes and a hard ruthlessness in his eyes that wasn't there in Allman Town.

Soon George was running regular blues sessions featuring the new big band and ska records that were beginning to be made in Jamaica and smuggled out without labels to supply the homesick London Jamaicans. Some weekends George might have as many as three sessions in various locations in the Black ghettoes of Shepherds Bush, Brixton and Notting Hill.

But the English residents in the ghettoes did not like this intrusion of noise and Black culture. They called the noise "an invasion of privacy" and "the sounds of jungle bunnies". The first racial skirmishes broke out, grew into an uprising, then a civil war. From his secure basement hideaway, George directed much of the strategy of the Black Notting Hill retaliation, venturing out only in the company of men armed with sticks.

One such excursion, they were confronted by a group of White thugs. George thought he recognized a policeman among the group, who had been harassing him recently trying to get some evidence to curtail George's activities. But George couldn't be sure that it was really him, since he wasn't wearing his uniform and helmet.

In any case, he didn't have much time to look at faces in the fight that followed. Just as George's group was gaining the upper hand, a police car rounded the corner and the police held and arrested George and two other of his mates who hadn't managed to escape. The police made no attempt to chase or hold the White thugs.

In court George and his mates were forced to accept a court-appointed White lawyer and, despite a plea of not guilty on the assault charge George was found guilty, especially on the strength of the testimony of a certain policeman, this time in uniform, who gave eyewitness testimony. The judge gave a stern lecture, which was widely reported in the British press, about those strangers who come into the British way of life and try to use violence to disrupt it. He also warned the Black community, via George and his convicted mates, that they should cease their aggression or face stiffer penalties.

George got four years. He served two and a half years of the bitterest humiliation he had ever experienced in his life. He was jeered and taunted by prison guards and White prisoners, called *"blackie"*, *"coon"*, *"nigger"* and *"wog"* and made to perform the most filthy tasks as daily duties. His fellow Black prisoners, of whom there were many, suffered in the same way. The experience entrenched his bitterness.

George had to start from scratch when he got out, to build himself up again. He had only his reputation as a good fighter, and used this to offer his protective services to three women, two Black, one White, in return for a percentage of their earnings. Certainly the percentage was large, but George saw to it that their accommodations looked good, and brought them a better class of customer than they were used to.

He had a two year run of luck. What ended it was a fight he had with Ricketts over the White woman. Ricketts wanted her. He got her and also a scar across his face from George's knife. That meant George had to go into hiding from Ricketts, who went to the police and reported George.

They finally cornered George, now down to his last penny in a scabby room in Islington. George fought so hard not to be captured, that the police also brought assault charges against George again. Another four years in Brixton Prison.

When he got out, his friend Roy who had been living in George's basement flat while he was in Brixton, was happy to agree to go in with George on his third attempt at survival,

England style. They moved from the basement with its unhappy memories, into one floor of a house in Notting Hill, which they fixed up into quite a comfortable refuge using the funds which Roy had put aside as rent for George while he was inside.

When they had done this, they went to Euston Station and picked up their first girl. Margot, she said her name was. How easy these White girls were. Margot became the source of George's income for one and a half years.

But the 'fuzz' wouldn't leave George alone. Especially because they wanted some information on the murder of a policeman by a friend of George's, and they were convinced George knew where he was hiding.

So they continued to harass George until one day they saw him on the Portobello Road and ran him down, saying he had stolen some T-shirts. When they caught George, they took him to a Greek man who, looking away from George's eyes, said Yes, it was George who had stolen his T-shirts. The policeman searched George and found his knife, and charged him with larceny and carrying an offensive weapon.

Just when George was going crazy trying to figure out who he could get to stand bail for him when Mr. Jones couldn't come to court any more, he remembered a Jamaican girl he had met with those rich Jamaicans who owned the Jamaican pattiy store on Portobello Road. "I work at the High Commission", he remembered her saying when he asked how come she knew those rich White people.

George found her in the High Commision office, but the con speech he had prepared to give her vanished when he saw that she was not only willing to help, but understood just why he needed her help and what he was up against. He hadn't expected her to be conscious, because she straightened her hair and talked like she was English.

But she was a good person and, George realized, 'decent', unlike any girl he had ever met in his life. She listened when he told her about his life and, surprisingly, she understood it from his point of view and didn't scorn him because of what she knew. George fell in love with her.

He knew his friends would laugh at him when he took her to a blues dance way across town in a rough area. They laughed, especially at her straight hair and innocent air. But George could see that under it all, they secretly envied him for being with such a nice decent girl. When he asked her how she felt about the people and places he introduced her to, she laughed and said she had long been wanting to know more about that part of Black London life.

She stood bail for him and in her clear, upper-class manner, gave the Magistrate no option but to agree to give George bail and release him into her respectable custody. The arresting policeman was angry that George had once again escaped his clutches temporarily. George wanted to make the distance permanent, to escape to Jamaica, for time seemed to be running out for him. She said no, running wouldn't help. He should stay and face the music. She would help him. George was tempted.

After all, she was here.

But then he had to be realistic. There was absolutely no future with this woman. She didn't even know herself as fully Black, or else she wouldn't still have a White woman's hairstyle, and speech and ways. What possible future could there be between him, an ex-jailbird and her, a society girl? But could he bear to leave her?

"Do you love me?" he asked her, in pain, fearing her answer, but strong enough to stand the negative.

"Yes," she had said, after a pause in which she searched herself fully.

But one night she threw a party at her fashionably hippy flat, and when George and Roy turned up, they and her were the only Black persons in the crowded room. George was extremely uncomfortable among these strange people of a group he did not care to mix with. They looked very upper class, and George did not speak that language.

When he tried to get her to pay him some attention, she behaved like he was just another friend of hers, nothing special, especially not as special as a certain young White boy with blonde curls with whom she spent a great deal of time talking.

George was not to know that the young White boy was only a friend who was having such bad emotional problems with his woman, that when he went home after the party he found that she had committed suicide in his bed. George thought the attention the White boy was receiving was the attention he should have been getting, and that she was embarrassed to let her White friends know that he was her man.

He waited until the party was over, till four in the morning when everyone had left, andthen he beat her up.

Not too bad to leave marks or seriously hurt her, though he wanted to hurt her as much as he was hurting. Just enough to get rid of his anger, sorrow and hurt, and to try and tell her what being a Black man's woman meant.

For he loved her.

Then he left.

He saw her only once again, when he went to her flat to take back the stereo set he had given her, so that he could cash it to pay his escape fare back to Jamaica. She said she understood. She was not angry with him, didn't even hate him. She understood that the beating she received had been deserved, just as much as he understood that it meant the end of what had been.

George escaped to Jamaica. He packed his duffel bag, took a train to Victoria Station and another to Heathrow Airport, where he walked up to the ticket desk and paid Four Hundred Pounds cash for a return ticket on the next flight to Jamaica. He waited eight hours in the Departure Lounge, then sat for another eight hours on the BOAC airplane, praying every minute that it would not crash, then giving God thanks with a huge sigh of relief when it landed safely at Palisadoes Airport in Kingston.

It cost an expensive Fifty Pounds for the taxi to Ocho Rios, then another Five Pounds for the car that took him over the broken, potholed road that was little more than a dry river bed , leading to the small village where his father used to live in the days when George was a boy, in the days before George stopped going to school to play by the river with other dropouts, in the days before George started stealing and selling the food growing on other people's farms, in the days before that big fight with the farmer that had made George run away to Kingston, where he got into all the trouble that made him run away to England.

The land was still there, and the house. The paint was faded and the edges of the house were broken, top to bottom. The yard was overgrown, and moss covered the grapefruit tree outside the verandah.

On the verandah sat an old woman. George got out of the car, opened the gate and walked up to the house.

"Who you is?" The old lady raised herself from the chair. "You look like Derek son. Is you?"

George was surprised. "How you know me? Who is YOU?" he asked her.

"I am Miss Elsie. I look after your father till him die. You father wait a long time for you, hope you would come home before he die. When he never see you come, he tell me to wait for you till you come. He say he know you will come home."

She held out her thin arms. "Come home."

And just like that, George came home.

There are still some people in the village who remember when George was a boy and the things he used to do. It has not been easy to be confronted by them, and to apologize for his past sins. But George knows that he has to be humble to live with his past, to live down his past.

When George looks up at how blue the Jamaican sky is and how golden the sunshine is on the green leaves of the trees, it is easy for George to be humble. When he sees the blue sky instead of the cold, grey sky through prison bars, George knows that he is a lucky man.

George built a chicken farm in the back yard, and sells the fowls to the Chinese grocery shop in Steer Town. Most days you will find George sitting under the grapefruit tree. There is no moss on the branches now, and the yard is neat and blooming. The house is painted and the roof fixed.

George fixed up a shed in the back yard as his own, and let Miss Elsie rent out his bedroom to provide them with a regular income. When Miss Elsie died, George found a quiet country girl and married her, and she in gratitude has raised three children and made a good home for George.

When he is resting you can usually find George sitting under the grapefruit tree, strumming on the guitar he found among the few things his father left. George likes to sing and play songs on his guitar. His friend, Nestor who also has a guitar, comes over sometimes to sit under the grapefruit tree and play music with him. Sometimes he and Nestor dream about writing a song that becomes a big hit that people dance to and sing. They laugh about this a lot.

George's London friends wouldn't recognize him now with his dreadlocks, his simple lifestyle, his ital food, and always beside him the Bible and the chalice full of fragrant ganja. Yes, George has come home.

But he never forgot that woman, the first and only woman he ever loved.

Funnily enough, she couldn't forget him either.

George, her first Black man.

HIS IMPERIAL MAJESTY, EMPEROR HAILE SELASSIE I

Emperor Selassie is the center of the philosophy that was first expressed by Elder Leonard Howell to answer the need felt by Jamaican descendants of enslaved Africans to re-connect with their home Continent. They were encouraged by Marcus Garvey, our first National Hero, to be inspired by the hope that one day they would return and restore Africa to be the home from which they were taken. It is legend that Garvey said African descendants should look to the coming of a special African King, who would lead that inspiration and movement.

For leaders like Leonard Howell, Bongo Watto and Prince Charles Emmanuel Wallace, the early founders of the main Mansions of Rastafari, Emperor Haile Selassie fulfilled Garvey's prophesy and their speeches, teachings and life work led to the growth and development of the Rastafari movement, lifestyle and philosophy,

Despite the opposition, rejection and frequent brutality experienced by the followers of these controversial leaders, Rastafari has continued to grow and become an international movement, especially with the help of the Reggae music produced by followers of the faith in songs that carried not only a new and hypnotic rhythm, but also a spiritual message of Black Christianity and Biblical morality.

Rising above many negative incidents and obstacles in past times, the Rastafari philosophy has today become accepted as an integral part of Jamaican life, admired and emulated by thousands and millions of all nations and races. Rastafari gave the world a new musical hero in Bob Marley, and there is no country on earth where he and his songs are not known and sung. The Rastafari declaration of ganja as a spiritual sacrament, has led Jamaica to acknowledge and legalize a thriving Jamaican cannabis industry, in which our country joins others around the world that have recognized and legalized the plant.

All this has happened because of the admiration by Jamaicans from Marcus Garvey, Leonard Howell, Alexander Bedward, Bob Marley and so many others since then of one very unique Ethiopian monarch, descendant of the Biblical King Solomon, in whose lineage Iyesos of Nazareth was born, and now manifested for the world to see as Emperor Haile Selassie I, a very special man elevated above so many other global leaders of this age, and highly honored by the poorest, most humble, most despised, but most influential Jamaicans - the RasTafari KElders, Empresses, Priests, Princes and Princesses.

PRAISE H.I.M.

Made in the USA
Columbia, SC
17 February 2024